The Love by Design series

Craving Him

Working It

Also by Kendall Ryan

When I Surrender

When I Break

The Impact of You

Resisting Her

Hard to Love

Make Me Yours

Unravel Me

All or Nothing

A Love by Design Novel

Kendall Ryan

ATRIA PAPERBACK
New York   London   Toronto   Sydney   New Delhi

ATRIA PAPERBACK
A Division of Simon & Schuster, Inc.
1230 Avenue of the Americas
New York, NY 10020

First Atria Paperback edition September 2014

ATRIA PAPERBACK and colophon are trademarks of Simon & Schuster, Inc.

For information about special discounts for bulk purchases, please contact Simon & Schuster Special Sales at 1-866-506-1949 or business@simonandschuster.com.

The Simon & Schuster Speakers Bureau can bring authors to your live event. For more information or to book an event, contact the Simon & Schuster Speakers Bureau at 1-866-248-3049 or visit our website at www.simonspeakers.com.

Manufactured in the United States of America

10   9   8   7   6   5   4   3   2   1

Library of Congress Cataloging-in-Publication Data

Ryan, Kendall.
    All or Nothing : a Love by Design novel / Kendall Ryan. — First Atria Paperback edition.
        pages   cm.
    (Love by Design ; 3)
    1. Fashion—Fiction. 2. Love stories. I. Title.
    PS3618.Y3354A79 2014
    813'.6—dc23
                                        2014018760

ISBN 978-1-4767-6464-1
ISBN 978-1-4767-6465-8 (ebook)

He was just too tempting, and all my defenses were weakened.

How could I not indulge in what he offered?

All or Nothing

1

"Ahhhhh . . ." A deep male groan broke from behind the closed door.

Sex noises seemed really out of place in a church. Call me old-fashioned, but I was certain of two things: One, doggie style should be reserved for the bedroom, and two, we were all going to hell. "Come on," I urged Braydon, tugging his tuxedo-clad elbow. "We can't listen to this."

"I'm not going anywhere." His feet remained planted to the floor, despite my efforts to shove him farther down the hall.

A loud, thundering moan vibrated the door.

My eyes jerked up to Braydon's. His mouth quirked up in a lopsided grin, showing off his perfect dimple. He lowered himself to the floor, leaning his back against the wall with his long legs stretched out in front of him, and crossed his feet at the ankles.

"What are you doing?" I hissed. *Shouldn't we give our friends some privacy?*

"Guarding the door." He shrugged. "I'm sure one of those photographers outside would love a shot of the action in there." He gestured with a nod toward the door of the church library where our friends were currently getting it on.

I couldn't argue with that. There was a fleet of paparazzi outside who'd give their left testicle to get a shot of the action today. This wedding was practically the event of the summer in Manhattan. World-famous male supermodel Ben Shaw's wedding to my best friend, Emmy, would be front-page news on the celebrity gossip sites.

I looked down at Braydon's stretched-out form. He was dressed in a tailored black Armani tuxedo, crisp white shirt, and sleek Italian leather shoes that tapered just slightly at the toe. His bow tie was hanging loose around his open collar, and he was sipping from a silver flask, watching me curiously.

"Come sit with me." He tapped the floor beside him with his knuckles. "Those shoes can't be comfortable." His eyes slowly lowered, wandering the length of my black strapless gown and all the way down to my strappy five-inch heels.

He was right again; I'd been in them for thirty minutes and already I could feel my toes becoming numb. The price of beauty. Sometimes it sucked being a girl. I sighed, not wanting to admit he was right.

"I won't bite, kitten. Unless you want it rough." He flashed his dimpled grin at me again and my stomach knotted.

Braydon tested my willpower like no one else. I'd sworn off men, so why did I want to take off my panties and give in to him? Lord, this wasn't healthy. Not one bit. I forced my eyes from his. Gazing into his navy blue depths felt entirely too intimate. He saw too much. I wondered if he knew just how much he got my heart racing. I'd met him last year through our mutual friends, Ben and Emmy. He was a sinfully sexy male model, often working with Emmy's soon-to-be husband, and trouble with a capital T.

Defeated, I slipped off my heels and sunk down on the floor next to him. Trying to maintain a sense of modesty, I arranged heaps of black satin and organza around my legs in the hallway of the church where my best friend was about to wed the man of her dreams. Pity party, your table of one is now available. I knew it was cliché, but weddings depressed me. Always have. I'd helped Emmy into her dress and fussed with her veil until it was just perfect. And now, I could only imagine what was going on in that church library, and the mess I'd have to clean up before their wedding ceremony even began.

"Ben wanted a quick fuck." Braydon shrugged like this situation was completely normal.

Oh, that was romantic. Men were disgusting. I rolled my eyes at him; I felt like sticking out my tongue, too, but I didn't. Weren't most people nervous before their wedding? Apparently Ben and Emmy were just horny.

But this was fucking ridiculous. Their wedding ceremony was scheduled to begin in twenty minutes, and I could see the stream of guests already filtering in and sitting with the assistance of the ushers. When Ben had come knocking at the door, looking for Emmy, I hadn't argued; I'd just helped her out of the one-of-a-kind white lace gown made just for her by Vera Wang, and let him inside the little library where we'd been getting ready.

His eyes had drunk her in, moving down from the little white bra and panty set to the pale blue garter around her thigh. "Fuck, sweetheart," he'd murmured.

The chemistry and intensity between them was impossible to ignore. It'd always been that way between them though. Ben had crossed the room in three long strides, stopping in front of her and watching her with a look of adoration. His hands had skated down her sides, gliding over her hips and thighs. His voice had been a weak whisper when he told her how beautiful she looked. My heart had twisted in my chest. It was obvious how much he loved her, despite how many times he'd messed up. You only found a love like that once in a lifetime. And as happy as I was that my best friend had found it, it only reminded me of how painfully alone I was.

As I sat trying not to listen to my friends go at it in the tiny church library, I wished it was me in that room with a white poufy dress pushed up to my ears and a man who was so deeply in love with me he couldn't wait another moment to be inside me.

"Is it true?" Braydon asked, passing me the flask.

"Is what true?" I accepted the flask and took a small sip. Mmm. I wasn't expecting it to taste good. Citrus vodka. My favorite.

"That bridesmaids are horny at weddings," he chuckled.

"Guess you'll have to be a good boy tonight to find out,"

I replied, taking a healthy swig from the flask before handing it back to him. "Zoey and Jenna are both single." So was I, but that wasn't happening. No thanks. I'd be leaving here tonight with my dignity intact.

His eyes lifted to mine. "There's someone else I had in mind, actually."

That little pang of nerves in my stomach was back. He needed to stop flirting with me. I wasn't interested. Sure, my body processed that he was sexy—he was a supermodel for goodness' sake—but my brain wasn't stupid enough to fall for his batting eyelashes and quips. I wasn't going to be another notch on his belt. "That's not happening," I deadpanned.

Braydon chuckled, the low rasp sliding from his perfect lips. He was like one of those jock-types in high school who thought the V on his varsity jacket stood for vagina. He was a total player, I was sure of it. "We'll see," he said.

"I'm a bitch to you. Why do you even like me?" I asked.

"I don't argue with my cock, sweetheart. And he seems to like you. In fact, he'd like to get to know you a lot better."

Good Lord! He couldn't say things like that to me. I wanted to tell him where to take his cock and shove it, but I was afraid of what might come out of my mouth.

His hand patted mine. It was meant to calm me, but any time he touched me little darts of heat fractured out from his fingertips and across my skin. It was disorienting. I pulled my hand away and tucked it safely into my lap.

We sat there in silence, passing the flask back and forth, listening to our friends' muted sex noises. God, it'd been entirely too long since I'd gotten any. I clamped my thighs together and groaned. I felt Braydon watching me and turned to meet his eyes.

"You need something, kitten?" His voice was deep and low. Too sexy for his own good.

"I'm fine," I squeaked out. "You good?"

"Oh, I'm fucking fantastic."

Finally, the door opened and Ben emerged, his hair thoroughly rumpled—from Emmy's wandering hands, no doubt. A giant smile was planted across his full mouth.

I rolled my eyes. "You two need to go. I need to get her dressed." I gestured to Braydon. "Go fix his sex hair."

Braydon saluted me. "You got it, boss."

The wedding ceremony was beautiful and heartfelt, perfectly representative of Ben and Emmy, just as I knew it would be. They had written their own vows and exchanged them in a tearful display in front of several hundred guests. It was beautiful to watch.

After a thousand photos and makeup touch-ups, we arrived at the reception at a beautiful, historic hotel overlooking Central Park. They'd certainly gotten lucky today. August in New York City could be brutally hot and humid this time of year, but it was mild, sunny, and perfect.

All through pictures, dinner, drinks, and dancing, I played the quintessential maid of honor. I was attentive to Emmy, smiled and made small talk with her loopy relatives from Tennessee, danced with her rather sweaty cousin, Randy Joe, and was fondled by her perverted Uncle Lou more than once.

I'd lied and told Emmy I was fine not having a date to her wedding—I'd reasoned that being the maid of honor meant I'd be too busy to entertain a man. But the truth was, watching Ben hold Emmy close on the dance floor and seeing the older couples swaying together made me realize it was pointless to lie to myself. Not that I had any viable date options. My recent prospects consisted solely of a string of lousy first dates, thanks to the Internet, with no real prospects on the horizon. My best friend's wedding only amplified my loner status. *Enter shame spiral.*

I wanted that deep, all-consuming love and acceptance when someone just got you. I didn't want just a boyfriend. I craved true intimacy and the peace of knowing I'd found my someone. I was tired of the game, and I wanted to settle down with a nice man. But something told me that working sixty hours a week as a scientist and shunning the entire male population wouldn't make it easy to find my happily ever after. I wasn't foolish enough to believe in fairy tales, but having a front-row seat to my best friend falling in love with a male model, traveling the world, and gushing about mind-blowing sex with a man who was allegedly hung like a baby elephant was making me hold out hope for my own Prince Charming. Possibly to my own detriment.

With my high heels pinching my feet, I headed for the exit, needing a moment to myself. The dance floor raged behind me, but my destination was one of quiet solitude. Emmy's mom stopped me in my path.

"Darling, I think we're low on champagne. There's more in the storage closet down the hall. Would you mind?"

"Not at all." It'd give me a reason to escape for a few minutes. Be alone and catch my breath.

"I'll escort her." Braydon appeared beside me out of nowhere. I'd noticed him throughout the night, quietly sipping his beer and keeping me in his sights but maintaining his distance.

His tone and the intense look in his eyes left little room for argument, so I merely nodded and turned for the exit. Making my way through the crowded ballroom, I felt Braydon's hand ghosting along the small of my back as he guided me. Little flutters of heat raced along my spine, pooling low in my belly. I turned down the deserted hallway, thankful for a moment of silence. Today had been exhausting. Not to mention, it wasn't the easiest thing in the world to be surrounded by two people who were so in love when my own love life was in the crapper.

We reached the storage room at the end of a long hallway only to find it locked.

"Dammit," I muttered, wrenching on the door handle.

"It's fine. We'll just find one of the catering staff and ask them to bring up more champagne." His hand closed around my elbow and an electric current zapped through me. It was as though his body knew mine and was calling to me. *What the hell was that?*

"Hey," Braydon said, lifting my chin to his. "Is everything okay?"

"Fine. Why?" I lied.

He lifted one shoulder. "You don't seem like yourself. Tonight, after that speech . . . I don't know. I wondered where my little firecracker had gone. . . ." His hand lifted to my upper arm and glided along my skin in slow, measured strokes.

He was incredibly perceptive. Too much so. But I couldn't have him getting to me. My maid of honor speech had been cut short when a lump of emotion had lodged in my throat, and I'd nearly broken down in front of everyone. I'd said a quick congratulations and ended it. Emmy and Ben seemed none the wiser, happily kissing and clinking their champagne glasses. I found it interesting that Braydon, of all people, had been perceptive enough to pick up on the change in me.

I sucked in a fortifying breath. I couldn't let him see how weak and alone I felt. "She's still here and will happily kick you in the balls if you decide to get too handsy." I glared at the hand he'd left resting on my bare shoulder.

He quickly withdrew the offending hand. "Glad you're back."

I swallowed down a wave of nerves, my heartbeat quickening as I realized we were all alone.

"You look stunning tonight. I should have told you earlier," he said.

My eyes lifted to his and I parted my lips to speak, to give him one of the sassy quips I was known for, but nothing came out.

"Shh, it's okay," he said, his palm cupping my cheek. "You don't have to be tough all the time, you know?"

I nodded slowly.

"I know you can take care of yourself, but who takes care of you, Ellie?"

He rarely, if ever, called me by my actual name, and the familiarity of it passing over his lips caused a little ripple of desire to dance in my belly. "No one," I admitted. "Men suck."

"I can't argue with that. Most men are assholes who behave like spoiled children."

I nodded slowly, glad we were on the same page. I thought he'd try to convince me otherwise, or at least tell me that he wasn't one of them. But he just stayed quiet, watching me with those gorgeous blue eyes of his, making my skin hum with nervous anticipation. *What were we doing?*

"I could take care of you tonight, make you feel good, if you let me," he whispered, his mouth just a few inches from mine.

My heart rioted in my chest. He was so good-looking, so sexy. I knew it'd be incredible. But the word *tonight* stood out to me. I was done with men who wanted one night with me. I supposed a string of failed dates and one-night stands would do that to you. I was looking for something more, a deeper, intimate connection; a real relationship. Not a one-night stand, not a guy who wanted nothing to do with me in the morning. Braydon had a way with words, I'd give him that. That didn't mean anything was going to happen, though.

"A few sexy words and you expect me to just hand over my panties?" I quipped.

"No. I'd prefer to peel those off you myself. Slowly. Savoring every delicious inch of skin I exposed."

My eyes slipped closed. My body was screaming at me to give in, to pull him into the nearest coat closet or restroom and let him have his way with me. To make this ache between my thighs go away. But my brain, ever in control, knew I couldn't do that.

"May I kiss you?" he whispered.

Temptation to kiss him flared inside me, unbidden and unwelcome. I'd been unconsciously watching the way his mouth moved when he spoke, as he took sips from his glass, fantasizing about how those full lips would feel against mine. Despite my body's urgings, I slowly shook my head.

"What are you afraid of?" he whispered. "Falling for me?"

I raised an eyebrow, looking at him like he'd grown a second head. "There's no chance of that happening," I scoffed.

"Then kiss me," he rasped.

"Why would I kiss you?" I asked, breathless yet fighting to remain in control.

"Because you want to." His statement was bold, direct, and sure. I hated how well he could read me.

"No, I don't," I murmured weakly. *Stay strong, Ellie.*

He chuckled softly. "Okay, kitten. Then let me kiss you. I want to see if you're still as feisty when that pretty mouth is occupied."

My silence was the only answer he needed.

He took my hand and dragged me the few paces to the women's restroom across the hall. In this quiet part of the hotel, it was deserted.

Braydon's warm palm cupped the bare nape of my neck, his thumb lightly rubbing against the soft skin. A chill darted down my spine. The simple contact from his hand was more than enough to ignite the fireworks between us into a raging inferno. His touch was firm, knowing, and decidedly confident.

With his hand still planted firmly at the base of my neck, he guided my body to his until our chests rested together. Our hearts pounded against each other, and I didn't know if it was from the adrenaline surge of arguing with him or the desire I felt flooding my system.

He certainly knew how to make my heart race.

All the bickering and heated arguments gave way to this moment. His blue eyes gazed fiercely down at mine and my tongue unconsciously darted out to wet my bottom lip. Braydon didn't miss the movement, his own lips parting as he softly inhaled.

I had no idea what he saw in me—what he must think of me—with my razor-sharp tongue and the neon sign above my head advertising how much I distrusted men. But in this moment, he obviously didn't care. He was every bit as wrapped up in this as I was. Maybe he was just horny, maybe it was our roles as maid of honor and best man at our best friends' wedding that had brought us to this moment . . . but regardless, there was no denying I wanted him to kiss me.

He was the king of mixed signals. He'd poked fun at me

all day, and now he was looking like he wanted to devour me from the inside out. The thought made my stomach flip. With my chest brushing his, I felt my nipples harden beneath my satin gown. I wasn't sure if he felt it too, but Braydon's eyes grew dark with his desire and began to slip closed. I didn't know what to make of him, but before I could even begin to sort out my feelings, his lips pressed tenderly against mine.

The softness in his kiss was unexpected. His fingers curled around my neck, fastening my mouth to his while he demanded I give in.

Knowing we were tucked away, with no chance of being discovered, I gave in to my desires. His fingers slowly knotted in my hair as he pulled me closer and deepened the kiss, his tongue lightly probing my mouth.

He was too sure. Too skilled. My libido immediately took notice, delivering a healthy dose of moisture to my panties. He turned something as simple as a kiss into a promise for sweaty, heart-pounding sex. If he kissed this well, surely he would be commanding and confident in the bedroom. Why did that thought excite me so much? I kissed him back with everything I had, my tongue sliding intimately against his as I tangled my hands in his hair.

After several moments, he slowly broke away, grinning against my mouth. "That wasn't so bad, was it?"

I parted my lips and drew a slow, shaky breath. I wanted to beg him to kiss me again, but instead I lifted one shoulder then dropped it in a noncommittal shrug. "It was okay."

He tipped his head back and laughed out loud. "You're

lying. I can see your body's response to me, kitten. Your panties are probably wet right now. Just from that one kiss."

I didn't deny it—I just held my eyes on his. Even in these insanely high heels, I had to tilt up my head to look at him. He evoked strange responses from my body. One minute I wanted to bite his head off for being a player, and the next I wanted to mount him and make him show me just how experienced he was between the sheets. God, I should be checked for multiple personalities. *Hold it together, Ellie!*

He bent down and his hands disappeared under the hem of my dress, skimming my naked calves and thighs. Chill bumps broke out in the wake of his smooth hands roaming along my skin. Was he honestly going to check if my panties were wet? And was I seriously going to let him? I knew I should stop him, slap his hands away, step back—something—but instead I stood there like a lovesick idiot, letting him manhandle me.

His fingers slid in through the sides of my panties and slowly twisted them, pulling them down my thighs. I knew I should say something. This wasn't okay, this wasn't me. Yet I watched in wonder as he let them fall to my ankles.

"Step out of them," he commanded.

I lifted one foot and then the other, leaving my panties haphazardly on the floor.

He slid one finger against my sex, and his mouth curved up in a grin. "You get really wet, don't you?"

Heat flooded my cheeks and my eyes dropped to the floor. *Oh, God.*

He tipped my chin up to meet his eyes once again. "Fuck, I like that. A lot."

I pulled in a shaky breath, relaxing into his touch.

His finger glided along my wet center and a whimper fell from my parted lips. It was laced with need, and Braydon recognized it immediately, his jaw tightening. His eyes danced as he looked into mine, and we tried to calm our ragged breathing.

"All this tension between us, my little firecracker, this electricity . . . don't you want to see what it will be like when I'm buried balls-deep inside you?" he murmured, his finger lightly rubbing my clit as his eyes met mine. I whimpered and bit my lip. Braydon continued watching me as though cataloging my every reaction as his finger continued to carefully circle the bundle of nerve endings so desperate for attention.

God, if he keeps that up, I'm going to explode . . .

"Can I taste you?" he asked.

All the blood rushed from my brain to my clenching sex, and I nodded wordlessly.

Walking us backward, Braydon guided me into one of the large bathroom stalls and slid the clasp into place, locking the door behind us. My heart pounded in anticipation.

Our eyes connected as he lowered himself to his knees in front of me, pushing my dress up around my hips as he went. Raw desire was reflected back at me as those beautiful blue depths penetrated mine. He hungered to put his mouth on me, and that thought alone drove me absolutely wild.

Balancing on precariously high heels with a poufy satin

dress lifted up around my waist, I braced one hand on the wall beside me for support.

"Put your hands here." He took my wrists, placing my hands on his shoulders instead. Then he slowly leaned forward, planting sweet kisses along my inner thigh. I writhed, trying to push myself closer, and balled my fists into his shirt.

"Hang on, baby. I'll take care of you. I promise."

His words instantly soothed me. I knew he would.

What in the world was happening between me and Braydon? I had no clue. But hell if I wanted to stop it. His tantalizing mouth moved to my other thigh, giving it the same treatment, trailing tender, sucking kisses all over the smooth flesh.

I gripped his shirt, my fingers sliding from his shoulders to his collar, to his hair, using it to tug him closer.

"Okay, enough teasing," he whispered. "You want to come?"

"Yes," I groaned out.

His mouth closed over my sex, sucking my swollen flesh into his mouth. He certainly wasn't shy. This wasn't the timid, noncommittal technique I was used to from most guys—a few flicks of the tongue before retreating to check a box. *Oral sex complete.* No, Braydon invested himself fully, pinning me in place and worshipping my lady parts until I was moaning and tugging against his hair to get him to ease up.

Hushed voices and footsteps came within hearing range. Braydon didn't stop his ministrations, despite me trying to wiggle away. His hands clamped down on my hips, holding me in place. The footsteps stopped just beside the door, and I peeked one eye open. I could see black Italian loafers and hot pink satin pumps under the doorway. *Holy shit!* It was Ben and Emmy.

Braydon and I froze, our gazes locking.

"Ben, I need you," Emmy whined.

"I know, baby. I want to fuck you so bad."

Emmy giggled. "Look. There are panties on the floor."

"Looks like we weren't the only ones with this idea," Ben said. "Our romantic wedding makes panties drop," he said as he chuckled softly.

After a moment's hesitation, Emmy asked, "Ellie? Is that you?"

Shit!

There was no use denying it. She could see my shoes, and since she'd picked out these strappy sandals for me, I knew we'd been spotted.

"Yeah, um, Braydon's just helping me, um, find my contact."

She hesitated just a moment. "You don't wear contacts."

Damn. I was hoping she'd be tipsy enough to overlook that fact.

"Yes, but I'm thinking of starting and I wanted to be sure . . ."

Braydon's hand squeezed mine and he shot me a sympathetic look. "We'll be out in a few minutes."

"Got it. We'll see you shortly," Ben said. I watched as their feet disappeared around the corner, and I sagged in relief.

"Thank you," I whispered to Braydon. My dumb ass had tried to convince Emmy I was getting contacts. Thanks to his quick thinking, or guy code or whatever, he'd gotten rid of them.

Without another word, Braydon's mouth returned to my core and I cried out at the unexpected onslaught.

Once my body was pulsing after its second release, Braydon slowly pulled back and lowered my dress into place, smoothing out the wrinkles over my hips with his hands. Then he rose and stood in front of me. A slow, lazy smile tugged one corner of his mouth up. "Hi," he whispered, his eyes dancing on mine like we were the only two in on a private joke.

I pressed my lips together to hide my smile. "We shouldn't have done that."

"You came, right?"

I nodded.

"Twice," he confirmed.

"I wasn't keeping track," I lied. It was two mind-blowing orgasms, more powerful than I'd ever experienced before.

"I was." His eyes locked on mine, possessive and dominant.

"That's not happening again."

"Yes it is."

Fuck.

I worked my bottom lip between my teeth while Braydon watched me curiously.

2

I waited for regret over my little tryst with Braydon to rise to the surface, yet it was strangely absent in the morning. I couldn't clear my thoughts of him. Maybe my pride was able to remain intact because we hadn't had sex and he'd remained fully clothed. I wasn't sure. I only knew I thought of last night with a warm and pleasant feeling.

After a quick shower, I combed my wet hair and opted for a low ponytail, jeans, and a cozy V-neck T-shirt. I had no one to impress. I was on my way to a casual coffee date with Ben and Emmy before they left for their month-long honeymoon. Of course, as Ben's best friend, Braydon would be there, too, but I refused to let things get weird between us after last night. I had nothing to be ashamed of.

When I arrived at the coffee shop, I spotted Braydon straightaway. He was waiting at the back of the line, fiddling with his phone. Gone were the tuxedo and shiny leather shoes of last night. Today he was in worn jeans slung low on his hips, beat-up navy blue Converse sneakers, and a light gray T-shirt that hugged his long, lean frame. He looked every bit as edible as the night before. His hair, unstyled, was missing the shiny pomade and was pushed up in the front in a casual yet sexy way. I wished I was immune to him, but seeing him standing there, looking like sex on a stick, it was obvious I was anything but. Damn hormones. I had no choice but to join him at the end of the line.

"Hi, kitten. How are you feeling this morning?"

"Uh-uh." I wagged my finger at him. "What happened last night is never happening again."

"Relax, babe. It was fun, right?"

I nodded reluctantly. No denying that. I'd replayed the way his messy dark hair had looked between my thighs, the way his mouth had devoured me, the sure way his fingers had stroked me inside. I couldn't believe I'd allowed him to go down on me, and that I'd done nothing in return to him and then fled. That wasn't supposed to happen between us. I felt like an idiot. Or the coolest chick ever. *Ha!* When I'd apologized later for leaving him in that state, he'd merely shrugged and said he had hands—implying that he'd take care of himself.

My heart throbbed painfully in my chest as he continued to watch me.

Tipping his head low to whisper near my ear, his warm scent greeted me. "I want *all* of you next time."

I shook my head. "Braydon, that's not happening again. I was just lonely and caught up in the moment. I'm changing teams. No more men for me."

"It's only a matter of time. I *will* be inside you."

A tiny whimper escaped my throat.

"Shh." His hand pressed against my lower back. "It's going to happen. Don't fight it. I promise it'll feel good."

My heart thumped steadily in my chest.

His firm touch guided me forward in line to order. The barista stared at me blankly. *Shit!* I couldn't get my mouth to work.

Braydon leaned down to my ear. "You like coffee?"

I nodded, my head bobbing on my shoulders.

"Two medium coffees, please," he ordered for us.

I was reduced to pointing and nodding. God, this man turned me into a pile of hormones and sex. I needed medical help. *Stat!*

After handing the barista some cash, and dropping his change into the tip jar, Braydon accepted the two cups of coffee and led me to a table in the back. After making sure I was seated, Braydon turned to me. "Would like you cream? Sugar?"

"Yes, please. Both."

I watched his cute butt as he strolled across the room to doctor up our coffees.

Emmy and Ben entered as Braydon was making his way back to the table. We shared hugs and stories from last night while Braydon went to stand in line again to order for the happy couple.

Once he'd rejoined us, sliding into the empty seat next to me, Emmy's mouth curved up in a grin. "I was just thinking about last night . . . you know, when you *lost your contacts*," she said, using air quotes.

I kicked her under the table.

"Ouch!" She bent down and rubbed her shin.

"Sorry. Reflex," I apologized weakly.

"Seriously, though, will you guys be okay while we're gone?" Emmy asked, her eyes darting back and forth between me and Bray.

Braydon's hand disappeared under the table and closed around my knee, giving it a playful squeeze.

"Of course," I stammered.

"Braydon will take care of her, won't you Bray?" Ben asked.

Braydon looked straight at me, his brilliant blue eyes fringed in dark lashes smiling at mine. "I surely will."

Emmy looked skeptical but shrugged. "With you two, I don't know if I'll find you in a closet tearing each other's clothes off or with Ellie ripping your throat out."

"I like it rough." The low growl emanating from Braydon's throat caused my nipples to harden against my bra. "I'm in." Braydon grinned.

"Not happening," I barked, taking a sip of my coffee. *Damn!* Too hot. I winced, pushing the paper cup away from me. Being near him was maddening. I wanted to lash out at him one second and fuck him silly the next. My mood swings were going to give me whiplash.

"Excuse us a minute." Emmy grabbed my hand and yanked me from the table, practically dragging me to the restroom.

"Ouch . . . sheesh." I wrenched my hand free, splaying

my fingers open and closed in an attempt to get some of the blood to return to the digits.

"You and Braydon . . . oh my God, tell me everything!"

I splashed cool water on my cheeks and washed my hands. Emmy handed me a wad of paper towel, watching me closely in the mirror.

"What the hell happened last night?"

"Umm . . ." I accepted the paper towels, drying my hands and blotting my face. I didn't know how to answer, what to say.

"Seriously, you better spill it. I tell you everything about me and Ben. Every single detail."

It was true. She did. I'd listened to every sordid tale and given her advice when they first started dating—and every time he'd done something foolish to mess it up.

"Did you guys get it on? I know that crap about contacts was a lie, so you better just come clean."

"We fooled around a little. We didn't have sex."

A slow smile curled on Emmy's lips. "Did you see his piercing?"

"What piercing?"

She blushed feverishly. "Never mind. So what in the world happened? You fight with him constantly."

"I know. I guess all that bickering gave way to sexual tension and, I don't know. I just stopped fighting it last night."

"Okay, so are you guys, like, hanging out now?"

"No. It was a one-time thing. A stupid mistake. I'm just glad I didn't let it go any further than it did."

I hadn't really opened up to Emmy about my lonely and miserable state. I hadn't wanted to rain on her parade. She was deeply in love, planning a wedding, a honeymoon, and running Ben's charity. She had a lot on her plate. And even though I hadn't said the words out loud, I thought, deep down, she knew I'd had a string of bad relationships and wanted something real. I was done wasting my time on Mr. Right Now. My heart was sick of all the games. I was looking for the real thing.

"Okay. So we're still Operation: All Men Are Dicks."

I nodded. "Correct."

"Okay, well, just so you know, Bray's not really a dick. He's actually a really good guy."

Yeah, a good guy who'd seduced me with flirty glances and dirty words and stripped me of my panties in a public restroom. But when I reflected on last night, he hadn't expected anything of me. He'd gotten me off—twice, as he reminded me—and then let me flee the scene. I chuckled at the memory. It was rather odd for a hookup. Not like most guys, who would've wanted something in return.

"What?" Emmy asked.

"Nothing. Let's go back out there before Ben sends in a search party after you."

"He's not that bad!" She smiled. We both knew he was, but she loved him and all his possessive, dominant ways too much to argue.

We rejoined the guys at the table and finished our coffees. Braydon kept quiet and sipped his drink, every once in a while lifting his blue eyes to mine. I pretended not to notice. Ben checked his watch and announced they needed to get going if they were going to make their flight. I was getting used to her busy travel schedule, but still, the idea of not seeing Emmy for a month was not something I looked forward to.

We gathered on the sidewalk for hugs and farewells, and all too soon Emmy and Ben were whisked away by their driver to head to the airport.

Braydon turned to me and smiled. "Shall I walk you home?" he asked.

"No." So much for manners and pleasantries. I knew if I gave him an inch, he'd take a mile.

"Afraid you'll invite me up?" He grinned, tucking his hands inside his pockets and rocking back on his heels.

"No. I just don't want you knowing where I live. How do I know you're not a creeper?"

His face turned serious, his eyebrows knitting together in concern. "You can trust me, Ellie. I'd never do something you didn't want. And I'd take care of you, you know."

I nodded. One second we were playful and sarcastic; the next he was turning the tables on me, deepening the conversation to places I couldn't let myself go. "I'd rather just be alone," I murmured.

He nodded, watching my closely. "Can't blame a guy for trying. Enjoy your day, kitten." He turned and strolled away, leaving me watching his strong back and the delectable way his muscles moved under his T-shirt. With one hand still stuffed in his pocket, his other pulled out his cell phone. He no doubt had a bevy of girls on his contacts list, ready and waiting to warm the spot in his bed that I refused to take. Which was exactly as it should be. I needed to move on from my little Braydon adventure.

3

The following days at work dragged by at a snail's pace. I'd worked hard to become a microbiologist at a pharmaceutical firm in Manhattan, and most days it was rewarding. I studied living organisms and watched how they reacted to different stimuli. The last several days, though, I'd felt more alone than ever. Sitting in my windowless lab, I grew lonelier and bitter. Emmy was away for a month in Tahiti. I had no man, no prospects, and not even a pet to snuggle with at night.

On the way home to Queens I stopped to pick up my favorite Mexican food from Mucho Amigo, hoping it would cheer me up. After carrying the Styrofoam containers to my fourth-floor apartment, I kicked off my shoes and placed my food on the coffee table. My loneliness was nothing a spicy chicken enchilada couldn't fix. I hoped. I checked my personal email messages on my phone while I grabbed a Diet Coke from the fridge. An email from Emmy entitled EMERGENCY caught my attention.

Ellie,

Hoping you can help. We just received a call from the building super-
intendent that there was a water-main break in our building. They've
stopped the leak, but he said our apartment flooded. I'm hoping you
can go to our place ASAP to dry out our wet belongings so we don't
come home to a mold infestation. We have plenty of towels on hand
to dry up the place. Use whatever you need. I'm so sorry, but please
know we appreciate it!

Thank you!

xo,

Emmy Shaw

P.S. How much do I freakin' love signing my new last name?!

Son of a—! There went my relaxing dinner plans. I stuffed
my uneaten dinner in the fridge, grabbed my purse and keys,
then scurried off for Ben and Emmy's, back in Manhattan,
double-checking that I still had their key on my key ring as
I fled down the stairs, the appetizing scent of my enchiladas
fading in the distance.

Their apartment was pitch black when I arrived. The
power must have been shut off when they'd gotten the leak.
Great. I felt along the wall and made my way into the kitchen.
I'd been here half a dozen times, but not enough to know the
place by feel alone in the absolute darkness. I pulled out my
cell phone and used the meager light to guide me. Locating
a couple of candles and a lighter inside a junk drawer, I instantly felt calmer with the low, flickering flames illuminating
the dark, eerily silent apartment.

I surveyed the damage, carrying a candle out in front of me. The living room rug squished under my feet. Not a good sign. The bedroom, home office, and bathrooms seemed unaffected. The damage seemed to be centered in the living room, where everything, including the couch and throw pillows, were damp. Great. How did I get a large sectional out of the apartment by myself? This was just fucking fantastic.

A scrape of metal outside the door caught my attention. The door handle jiggled once, then twice, and a man's voice cursed. I'd locked the door behind me, but someone was clearly trying to get in. I'd seen too many scary movies with a girl alone in the dark in an unfamiliar place. Every hair on my body stood on end, and my hands shook with fear as I darted for the kitchen and drew a knife from the butcher's block. The door opened and I sprung forward, the knife out in front of me.

"Holy fuck!" the man swore loudly, guiding my knife-wielding arm away from his midsection and pinning me to the wall. "Kitten? Is that you?"

"Braydon?" I asked, peering at the handsome intruder in the faint light.

"Yeah. It's me." He turned me to face him, still holding my arm. "If I release you, you promise not to stab me?"

"Braydon! Stop it. Of course. I thought you were a serial killer."

He removed the knife from my grasp and set it on the nearby console table beside Ben's door. "Still, let's set this over here until you're feeling less stabby."

"What are you doing here?" I asked.

"I got a call from Ben. About the flood."

"I got an email from Emmy."

We watched each other for a few heartbeats in silence. Being near him again in the darkened, silent apartment sent a rush of awareness skittering over my skin. I remembered how his full mouth felt on mine, the insistence and gentleness of his kiss. I was glad the room was too dim for him to notice my cheeks turn pink and my hands begin to shake.

"You okay?" He reached out a hand to steady me, gliding it along my upper arm.

"Yeah. Sorry. I just . . . got a little light-headed. The power's off and you scared me."

"I'm sorry, kitten," he whispered, the deep timbre of his voice soothing me.

"It's fine." I turned away from him, unwilling to let myself get sucked into his orbit. Yet again. The other night was embarrassing enough. I'd come undone so easily for him. Good thing he didn't know that no man had ever had such a powerful effect on me.

"How bad is the damage?" he asked, following me into the living room.

"It's mostly centered in the living room. I think the couch is ruined. And the dining room floor's a little wet, too."

"Cool. You want some wine?"

Cool? I spun around to face him. He'd ventured into the kitchen and was raiding their wine cabinet. *What the hell?*

"I can't see what's what in the dark. How picky are you?"

"Um . . ." *Was he insane?*

"White or red?" he asked.

"We shouldn't. We're here to help, right?"

"Oh, we definitely are. I'm ordering us a pizza, too. You hungry?"

"Starving, actually," I admitted, my stomach grumbling at the mere mention of food and the thought of the uneaten enchilada in my fridge at home. Mmm, pizza sounded fantastic. "What about cleaning up?" I asked, looking from him back to the soggy living room.

Braydon shrugged. "I'll call someone to come remove the couch, rug, and whatever else tomorrow . . . but since they lured both of us here, I think we should relax and have something to eat. Ben has the best wine collection, too. He gets cases of this shit flown in from Italy. He's friends with the owner of a vineyard outside of Milan. Trust me, you'll want some."

I watched as he set two wineglasses and a bottle on the counter and began pulling open drawers in search of a corkscrew.

"It's in here." I pulled open the third drawer on the right and produced the fancy compressed opener I'd seen Emmy use.

"Sexy and talented. Thanks." He took the device from me and quickly opened the bottle, pouring a healthy measure into each of our glasses. "To water-main breaks." He lifted his glass to mine.

I smiled at him, feeling the tension and stress of my day

melt away just from his closeness. He had one of those magnetic personalities; he was so laid back, like nothing ever
bothered him. I found it refreshing and extremely intoxicating. I could use a dose of that in my life. I was wound so damn
tight most of the time. I took a sip of the wine and felt it warm
a path down my throat and into my belly.

"Since the sofa is out, shall we lounge in the bedroom?"
He winked.

"Oh, I don't think that's a good idea," I said with a snort.

"Why, gorgeous?" He leaned in close, brushing his nose
along my jaw and inhaling slowly. "Afraid of what might
happen?"

I rolled my eyes and followed him to the bedroom. Braydon situated candles on the dresser and bedside tables, pro-
viding a nice glow for the room. "What do you like on your
pizza?"

Honestly, I wasn't picky when it came to pizza, but I
blurted, "Sausage and extra onions." That would ensure I
wouldn't be tempted to kiss him again later. I'd have breath
from hell, thanks to those toppings. *Genius, Ellie.* I gave myself a mental pat on the back.

He shot me a curious glance.

While Braydon called in our order, I sat on the edge of
the bed, trying not to feel too out of place, alone with a man
I'd unabashedly got it on with last weekend, sitting on my
friend's bed in their dark, utterly silent apartment.

He kept our wineglasses filled and thankfully the conversation flowed as well. We sat cross-legged on the bed, shar-

ing an entire large pizza and two bottles of wine. And he was right. Ben had the best wine.

"So . . . do you like being a model?"

He nodded, taking another bite of the pie. He hadn't complained once about my choice in toppings. Smart man. "Yeah, it's not bad."

"Do you travel a lot?"

He shook his head. "New York's my biggest market. I tend to do a lot of print work and not as much of the international stuff, like Ben does."

Good to know. I could never handle being with a man who traveled that much. Not that I should even be entertaining such thoughts. Braydon was never going to be mine. I blamed the errant thought on the wine.

Once I was thoroughly full and tipsy, I fell back against the mountain of pillows piled at the headboard. I was full and nicely buzzed—an altogether pleasant combination. "I could stay here forever." *Oops.* I hadn't meant to say that out loud.

Braydon lay down next to me, bringing his palm to my cheek, his thumb gliding along my cheekbone. "You're awesome, you know that?"

"How so?" I mumbled.

"You're so chill, so easy to be around. You're not afraid to be yourself. Fuck, you're not afraid to eat more pizza than I did."

I slugged his shoulder lazily. "Hey! Way to make me feel self-conscious."

"I'm just impressed, that's all." He grinned his beautiful

lopsided grin, which lit up his whole face. The one that I was powerless against. Dammit.

"Don't do that." I squished his cheeks between my thumb and forefinger.

"What?"

"Flash that panty-dropping grin at me."

He chuckled, low and deep in his throat. "Most girls like that, kitten."

"I'm not most girls."

"I've noticed."

"Oh yeah? What else did you notice?"

"Hmm." His thumb stroked my jawline softly. It felt incredible. "How good you taste. Your scent. The way your body feels when you come. How it felt when you dug your hands into my hair."

My body responded to his voice by breaking out in chill bumps, my heart thumping quickly in my chest. His way with words was too much. He was too bold. Too confident. My poor libido couldn't take it.

"What do you remember?" he whispered softly.

A thousand images flashed through my brain. Braydon's hands skimming up my thighs. My panties dropping to the floor. His hands on my hips as he guided me into the stall. His tongue sliding against mine. The way his stiff tuxedo felt against my hands, and his soft hair between my fingers. "Your, um, pretty blue eyes and messy hair," I croaked.

He smiled widely. "Yeah?"

"Yeah." I nodded.

He leaned toward me slowly, giving me the chance to pull away. Only I didn't. I wanted to feel his mouth on mine again. I let my eyes drop closed and awaited contact. He didn't disappoint. His soft, full mouth pressed slowly to mine, his lips damp and parted. Our tongues touched once, twice, as he kissed me slowly. It made me want more. Pushing my hands into his hair, I angled my mouth closer, allowing him to deepen the kiss. His tongue swept against mine, dancing so knowledgeably and intimately that I was lost to him.

He pressed down on me, guiding me to the mattress so he could move on top of me. Suddenly realizing whose bed we were on, I pushed against him. This was wrong. "Stop, we can't."

"What's wrong, kitten?" he murmured against my neck, pressing damp kisses along the column of my throat.

"This is Ben and Emmy's bed." I pressed a palm flat against his chest, putting some distance between us.

He looked around like he was noticing our surroundings for the first time. Then he rolled off me and we lay side by side. "Let me take you home then."

"I can't. I'm sorry. This just isn't me."

He pressed a palm to my cheek, giving it a careful pat.

"I didn't mean to lead you on. I just can't do this."

His thumb lightly rubbed my cheek and his other settled against my hip. "You had fun the other night, right?"

"Yes," I admitted.

"Let me ask you something." He hesitated just a moment, his thumb lightly caressing my skin. "You feel this between us, right? This . . . connection?"

I blinked at him, refusing to answer. Of course I did. I'd be dead not to.

"We owe it to ourselves to give in to this. It's not always like this, you know? This chemistry we have. And I know you feel it, too." He swallowed, continuing to watch me. "I know you've sworn off men, so I'm not asking for anything in return. No commitment. No strings. Just us. Exploring this. Giving in to this sexuality between us."

Original. A man who wanted casual sex without any chance of commitment. "Are you high? What in the world makes you think I'd be interested in that type of arrangement?"

His eyes locked on mine. "You can't deny the chemistry between us. Imagine how good it will be when we fuck."

I inhaled swiftly, biting my lip to keep from whimpering.

Braydon continued, "Sex and intimacy is a physical need. An ache all of us have. I could fulfill that for you."

I remained silent while I contemplated his words. On the surface they made sense. I had physical needs. My vibrator usually satisfied those. For the most part. Sort of. But Braydon was gorgeous. And funny. And sexy. And he certainly wasn't cut out to be my Mr. Right, so there'd be little harm in indulging in whatever this was with him. Right?

"One taste wasn't enough, kitten," he growled.

Our eyes connected and I searched for meaning behind

his proposal. Why did he want me? And why did he want sex but not a relationship? What was that wounded look he worked to cover with his sexy bravado?

I knew this was wrong on so many levels. This was Braydon, male model and player extraordinaire. He was so far out of the realm of anyone I'd consider dating. But even as the thoughts tumbled inside my head, I knew that wasn't what this was. He wasn't asking to date me. And just once, I wanted to do something crazy. Act on my body's hidden desires for a man so devastatingly beautiful I'd want the lights on during sex—cellulite be damned—just so I could watch him come apart. I wanted to be naughty. To have an adventure that I'd remember fondly for years to come. And Braydon seemed all too happy to oblige me. Maybe it was the wine that had left me hazy and warm, but his idea didn't sound that bad.

He mistook my silence for acquiescence and leaned in to kiss me again, his lips softly molding to mine, then growing more demanding as the intensity between us ramped up. My arms circled his neck, my fingers roaming into his hair, and I pressed my body to his. His hips pressed to mine and I felt his heavy erection nudge against my belly. I pulled back just a fraction.

"Bray . . ." I breathed, pressing a palm to his chest. I didn't know what I was asking for, but the needy quality to my voice was a dead giveaway.

"I don't mean to get you so riled up," he chuckled.

"You don't."

His fingers pushed my hair back from my face and remained buried in my hair, lightly massaging my scalp. "I can see your pulse fluttering in your neck, the blush coloring your chest. I excite you."

"You scare me," I admitted softly.

"You want me to fuck you. To teach you the ways a man can pleasure your body."

I sucked in a breath and held it, shocked by his words. He did excite me. Possibly more than any man had ever before.

I couldn't believe I was actually considering this—hanging on his every word. This wasn't me. But after a string of bad first dates, lousy sexual episodes, and so many run-ins with my vibrator that I needed to replace the batteries—his offer was intriguing. I couldn't look away. His deep blue eyes gazed into mine so adoringly. He was mesmerizing. Utter male perfection.

"It's intoxicating knowing how feisty I get you." He brought his hand to my jaw and glided the back of his knuckles along my cheek. Shivers slipped down my body at the soft contact. No one had stroked my jawline like that before. So gentle, so soft. His touch was addictive.

"What do you want?" I found my voice, however shaky.

"Me and you. Pleasing each other. Giving in to this."

"You just want to sleep with me?" I wanted to hear him say it. I doubted he was offering to take me out and wine and dine me.

"Among other things."

"Like a one-time thing?" I held my breath for his response.

"Once wouldn't be enough, and we both know that."

Oh. The ache between my thighs intensified.

"Let's not overthink this." His fingers whispered against my skin.

I sat up on the bed, needing to distance myself from his sweet touch before I did something I might regret. I drew a deep breath, trying to clear my head from the wine and simultaneously ignore the ache between my legs that his presence alone inspired. "You're suggesting a friends-with-benefits type of arrangement?" I asked, pressing my fingers to my temples. I wished I hadn't drunk so much. My brain felt numb and heavy.

Braydon sat up beside me, watching my reaction. After a moment, he reached for his glass of wine and took another sip. "Hmm." He swirled the wine in his glass. "I prefer something more original. Pleasure pals . . . bed buddies . . ."

I smiled despite the insane conversation we were having. "Fuck friends."

"If you like."

"I don't know . . . I don't think I can do that. . . ." I said softly.

He took my hand. "Don't answer tonight. Let me take you home and tuck you into bed."

I nodded. Sleep sounded heavenly. I'd had too much wine. Too much pizza. Too much hormone-fueled conversation with a devastatingly handsome man. My body wasn't used to this.

"What time do you get off work tomorrow?"

"Six," I responded without thinking.

"I'll come by at seven with dinner. We'll discuss our arrangement then."

Our arrangement? "Okay," I agreed, sleepily, wondering what in the world I was actually agreeing to.

Someone had stolen my brain and replaced it with a pile of goo. I couldn't concentrate at work. I could barely form cohesive sentences. I'd dropped several petri dishes, spilled a specimen, and contaminated another sample I was working with. I'd consumed way too much wine for a Wednesday night and had woken up late and hung over. I'd gotten ready in a hurry, and as a result my hair was flat and dull and the dark circles under my eyes made me look like a zombie on crack. At lunch, I'd been so distracted, I'd picked at my food and dropped a huge glob of tuna salad on my shirt. Which led to me spending twenty minutes in the restroom trying to clean the stain, all while cursing myself out that I'd eaten smelly old tuna fish for lunch when I was supposed to see Braydon that night. I'd have to get home a little early to change my shirt and brush my teeth. Maybe touch up my makeup. And shave. Oh God, this was exactly why he wasn't healthy for me. He sent my brain into overdrive. I hadn't felt butterflies like this since I was in tenth grade and got felt up for the first time.

I'd replayed in my head what I would say to him a million times. Of course I'd refuse his offer. I was flattered, sure, but I couldn't actually go through with it. I'd just have to make him understand. Braydon, though I'd known him only a short time, could be very persuasive. And that's what scared me most. I couldn't let myself get sucked into his world.

I fumbled with the dial on my microscope, cursing loudly when I couldn't get the damn thing to cooperate.

"Are you okay?" my boss, Lydia, asked. She was looking at me with a concerned look, her wire-rimmed glasses balancing at the end of her nose. Lydia was a great boss. Smart as a whip, patient, and a great advocate for our department to receive the funding and training we needed to perform. I loved working for her. But we never discussed our personal lives. Ever. Aside from a simple "How was your weekend?" And I didn't plan to start now. "You seem distracted today," she said.

"I'm fine," I lied. I focused on the task in front of me, hoping she'd let it drop.

"I've worked with you long enough to know when something's wrong." She removed her glasses and set them on the table beside her. Her brown eyes crinkled in the corners as she gave me a sympathetic smile. "You can talk to me, you know."

I frowned and rubbed my forehead. I had a pounding headache from thinking about this arrangement with Braydon. "It's nothing. Just guy problems."

"Ah. I see." She nodded, her eyes weary and wise, like she'd been around long enough to know all about such matters. "Do you want to talk about it?"

I inhaled deeply and released it slowly. "No. But thank you for the offer." How did you tell your boss that a sexy male model wanted to become your . . . what did he call it again?

Oh yeah, *pleasure pal*. No, I wouldn't be explaining that to my boss. I wanted to keep my job, thank you very much.

She replaced her glasses and patted the back of my hand. "I'm sure you'll figure it out, Elizabeth. You're a very smart girl." She was one of the only people who called me Elizabeth and not Ellie.

I smiled weakly. I didn't feel so smart. I felt as if I was back in high school, complete with sweaty palms and a stomach full of nerves at the thought of the football captain wanting to ask me out. Scratch that. Braydon didn't want to ask me to go steady. He just wanted me naked and ready in the backseat of his car.

Shit.

These thoughts weren't helping me focus. "I didn't sleep well last night. I had to help a friend with a leak in her apartment." At least that part was true. Crap. Hopefully Braydon followed through on his promise to remove the soggy belongings and have the apartment aired out. Crappy friend that I was, I hadn't thought about that again since last night.

Lydia nodded. "Okay. Well, if you need to leave a little early this afternoon—recharge your batteries—you be sure to do just that."

"Thank you. I think I will." Another reason why I loved my boss.

I thought getting home early would be a blessing. Instead it just meant I had more time to sit around worrying before Braydon was due. I felt caged up inside my apartment, so after cleaning every room thoroughly I decided to change into a sports bra, T-shirt, and shorts and go for a jog. I figured I'd still have time to shower and get ready before he arrived. Pushing my muscles into action, with loud music blaring in my ears, was exactly what I needed. I felt sluggish at first—too many indulgences last night—but soon found my rhythm and pounded out three miles. When I arrived back home, my head was slightly clearer. Maybe I could do this with Braydon. Give in to my body's yearnings. Have a fun adventure. You only live once, right?

I turned the shower on as hot as I could stand it and let the water beat down on me. I scrubbed myself thoroughly, shampooed and conditioned my hair, and shaved my legs for good measure. I dressed in jeans and a T-shirt, refusing to primp for him. Refusing to pretend this was some type of date. He'd made it clear that we wouldn't be dating.

When Braydon arrived promptly at seven, my heart jumped into my throat. I answered the door and found him standing there, dressed casually in jeans and an old band T-shirt. His style was cute. Relaxed and vintage. I liked it. A lot.

"Hi," I said, pulling open the door wider.

"Hiya. Can I come in? I have Thai food." He held up a brown paper sack. "Of course it occurred to me that you might not like Thai, but you seem like an adventurous girl, so I went with it."

"Thai is fine. And please, come in." I motioned him forward and led him into my tiny kitchen. After gathering plates, utensils, and drinks, we carried the whole lot to the small round table in my breakfast nook.

"Nice place," he commented, looking around. I'd never officially given him a tour, but I was just trying to avoid that awkward moment when we ended up in my bedroom staring at the bed. I doubted I'd have a witty comeback when he suggested we christen it.

"Thank you. It's cozy."

Braydon opened each package and my stomach grumbled as I inhaled the mouthwatering aromas greeting me. There was roast duck, stir-fried vegetables in fragrant curry, sticky jasmine rice, and several different noodle dishes.

"Did you invite a hockey team over and forget to tell me?" I joked.

"I wanted to be sure I ordered something you would like." He flashed those pretty blue eyes at me, and my skin heated. He was thoughtful. That did not help my case against him.

Thankfully, scooping heaps of food onto my plate provided a good distraction from his prettiness.

"So, what do you do?" he asked, taking his time to arrange his food artfully on his plate. Gosh, was he going to gift wrap it or eat it?

"I'm a microbiologist at a pharmaceutical firm downtown."

"Shit, seriously? Did you go to school for that?" His mouth hung open, waiting for my answer.

"Yeah. I have a bachelor's degree in biology and a master's degree in microbiology."

His eyes widened. "Damn, girl. So, what does a sexy-as-fuck microbiologist do all day?"

Me? Sexy? I was pretty sure I had curry sauce smeared on my chin. I wiped my mouth with a napkin before answering. "I look at tiny organisms under a microscope. It's super exciting." I rolled my eyes for effect. I actually quite enjoyed my job and the challenge of it, but it usually bored people when I went into detail, so I kept it light.

"Do you get to wear one of those white lab coats?"

"Yep. Sure do. I examine cell reproduction, run studies on diseases, watch how different bacteria react to stimuli. . . ."

"Mmm, smart girls are sexy." He grinned again, flashing me his dimple that I was becoming a teeny bit obsessed with. I took another bite of roast duck to distract myself.

After dinner, Braydon insisted on helping me load the dishwasher, and then we sat down on the sofa side by side like two nervous teenagers. Actually, I was a nervous wreck, but he seemed calm, cool, and collected, kicking his feet up on the old trunk in front of my couch and throwing his arm across the back of the sofa. He hadn't brought up anything the entire night about our arrangement. The entire reason he was here, I thought. Instead, he kept up a steady conversation, leaving me waiting in wonder, the anticipation growing more and more with each hour that passed. Seriously, I was not a patient person and the wait was eating me up inside. Was he going to try to make a move on me? Had he changed his mind? Was he still attracted to me? Maybe I should have dressed sexier, curled my hair. . . .

"So tell me more about this arrangement," I asked finally, unable to wait any longer. Even if I was going to turn him down, something in me wanted to know what exactly he was proposing.

Braydon's mouth quirked up in a smile. "Are you ready to discuss that now, miss?"

I nodded slowly. Had he been waiting for me to bring it up the whole time? Was his silence on the topic meant to drive me crazy? Oh, he was good. He was damn good.

"What would you like to discuss?" he asked, his voice dropping lower as he turned to face me on the couch.

"How would it, um, work?" Ugh, why did I sound so breathless? I should tell him and his damn pleasure-pals arrangement to take a hike. But something in me couldn't. I needed to see where this was headed. I had no self-control when it came to this man.

"However we want it to. I'd like to see you a few times a week. We could have a meal, like tonight, and then enjoy each other's company." Smooth of him. But I'm pretty sure he meant *enjoy my vagina*. I suppressed a hot shiver and continued watching him.

"But we wouldn't be dating. There'd be no commitments." My heart clenched as I said the words out loud. I waited for him to correct me, to smooth things over, but that didn't happen.

"That's right. No expectations of each other. What I'm proposing is that we give into our baser instincts. Let go of inhibitions and discover each other."

I shook my head, fighting the urge to roll my eyes. I pulled in a deep breath and released it slowly. Inside my brain was an extreme game of Ping-Pong. I wanted this, yet I didn't. I was so back and forth. I held up a hand, needing a moment to think. I'd sworn off men, right? "Excuse me, I'm just having a problem with your gender lately."

He continued to watch me closely. "I know what you're doing. You put up this front, you say that you don't want a man. It's only because no one's been able to properly take care of you."

"And you think you can?" His confidence was a huge turn-on.

"I know I can. And I will. You just have to let me. Submit to me."

I wanted to argue, to tell him I was a strong, independent woman; that I didn't submit to anyone. But the words lodged in my throat, refusing to budge. "I seriously don't see what's in this for me."

"You have to feel this between us," he whispered, his blue eyes shining with his desire.

I hadn't felt a connection this deep with someone in a long time, maybe ever, but he couldn't know that. I stayed quiet and Braydon lifted my hand from my lap, interlacing our fingers and stroking the inside of my palm with his fingertips in featherlight strokes. Every touch from him felt deliberate. I was quickly becoming addicted to every little thing he did. He made my heart flutter. Silly little organ. It didn't know what was good for it.

I realized with perfect clarity that my body wanted this. Wanted to have a sexual adventure. And he was the perfect candidate to have a fling with. He was sexy and discreet. As far as I knew he hadn't breathed a word of our little postwedding romp to Ben or Emmy. And he turned my body into a puddle of hormones. There was no denying that. If I were going to have an affair, why not do it with a man who knew what the hell he was doing?

He leaned closer, bringing one hand behind my neck and knotting his fingers in my hair. "You want me to kiss you again," he said, as if it were a statement of fact. But the tenderness in his tone was unexpected and calmed me instantly. It was crazy how one minute he could rile me up with his talk of "discovering" each other, then turn me on just by touching my hand, then reel me into his world so completely that I couldn't look away, couldn't even blink.

One thing was certain. I wanted more. I wanted to see where this could go. There was something magnetic about him. His charm. His personality. Shit, his *tongue*. That was surely illegal in like forty-nine states. I might as well take advantage.

My disappointing sexual experiences so far had a lot to do with my consideration of his proposal. The few boyfriends I'd had couldn't have satisfied me if I'd drawn out a treasure map of my vagina with an X-marks-the-spot for my clitoris. Even when the sex had been decent, I'd always craved something more. A man who would take charge. Who knew instinctively what my body craved and gave it to me ruthlessly without me having to ask. I loved the idea of being manhandled a bit. Taken over. The idea alone made me wet.

My whole life was well ordered, from my daily jogs to my job that was actually an exact science, with rules and standardized processes to follow. No wonder I wanted a dirty, risqué adventure in the bedroom. My body battled with my brain. I shouldn't want what Braydon was offering. Then again, I was missing both the emotional connection of a serious boyfriend and a satisfying sexual relationship in my life. I knew with Braydon I'd be 50 percent of the way there. Not bad odds.

"What other questions do you have in that head of yours, kitten?" He stroked the furrowed spot between my eyebrows with his thumb.

I shook my head. "I don't know." I'd never had a pleasure pal, so I was totally at a loss about what to ask next. "Wait." I sat up straighter. "Will you be, like, dating other girls during this arrangement?"

"Hmm. Good question." He set my hand down in my lap. "What do you think?"

I chewed on my lip. He was asking me? "I don't know. I mean, I'm not dating anyone else right now, but . . ."

He shook his head, his eyes locking on mine. "Once I've been inside of you, you're mine. No one else gets to touch you. Do you understand?" That was ridiculous. We weren't dating and he wanted to lay claim to me like some dominant alpha male? I was a confident, successful woman. I didn't play games. So why was my head nodding in agreement to his absurd proposition?

A slow, easy smile spread across his mouth. "That's a good

girl, kitten. I promise I'll take care of you." He pushed my hair back from my face and watched my eyes. He reached for my cell phone and programmed his number in, then called his phone. Smooth.

"If I can't have anyone else inside me, as you so eloquently put it, then neither can you."

His eyes danced on mine. "No problem. If anyone tried to put something inside me, I'd break their fucking jaw."

"Braydon!" I slapped his shoulder playfully. "I mean you've got to keep it in your pants, mister. No other girls."

His mouth twitched in a smile. "I have quite a sexual appetite, lovely. Are you sure you can handle me?"

I bit my lip and nodded, heat crawling up my chest.

"I don't want to create an imposition for you." His hand circled my hip, his large fingers reaching all the way to my spine.

My nipples instantly hardened as my body responded to his nearness and his scent. A mixture of spicy cologne and clean soap. I wasn't sure what would happen next, but Braydon, ever the gentleman, rose from the couch. "You're tired. I should probably go."

"Oh." I stood too quickly and suddenly felt light-headed again. His hand on my elbow steadied me.

"Are you okay?" he asked.

"You're leaving?"

His features softened as he gazed down at me. "I can read the indecision all over you. Your body wants this. Your brain isn't sure." He already understood me so well, it was impossible to argue. He leaned closer, his lips brushing my neck. "And when I fuck you for the first time, I want you to be certain. I want there to be no questions in your mind. I want you begging me to penetrate you. I want your hand guiding me inside you." He pulled back to measure my reaction.

My knees trembled as I reached out to grip his bicep for support. Bad idea. The warm, solid muscle under my hand made me question everything. Should I invite him to stay? See where things went? I chewed on my bottom lip, the words on the tip of my tongue. But he was right . . . I was hesitating, not quite brave enough to take what I wanted. Stupid brain.

His mouth captured mine in a hungry kiss, his teeth nipping at my bottom lip, and when my mouth parted, his tongue stroked mine hypnotically.

Pushing his hips toward mine, he succeeded in aligning our bodies from chest to thigh. I could feel the way his tense erection strained against his jeans, and, all too aware that he'd touched me but I hadn't yet touched him, I reached out to rub the front of his pants. I wanted to feel him and his manhood. His hand caught my wrist and lifted it away from the front of his jeans. Pressing a kiss against my wrist, he shook his head. "Greedy little girl."

I swallowed roughly, needing to make light of my wanton behavior. "There's nothing worse than popping the hood and finding inadequate equipment underneath." I dared a peek down at his crotch, unable to hide my smirk.

"I think you'll be more than satisfied with my equipment, miss."

"Then let me see." I rubbed against him again, loving the steely feel of his warm length encased in denim.

He shook his head. "You will. But not tonight. How about I just taste you instead? I want to lick your pussy again," he whispered.

My fingers reflexively tightened around his arm. How could I say no to that? My head gave a little nod and he quickly led me to my bedroom.

When we reached the darkened room, his fingers laced between mine again, the move possessive and intimate. I liked it way too much. We kissed for several minutes, standing in the center of my bedroom until I felt Braydon's fingers find the button on my jeans. I wouldn't stop him now. Couldn't. My body wanted this.

Pushing my jeans and panties down from my hips, Braydon suddenly lifted me, tossing me onto my mattress. His strength was unexpected, and I let out a small squeak when I hit the bed.

Grinning his impish little grin, that sexy dimple taunting me so adorably, he leaned down and kissed my navel. "This okay, baby?" his breath whispered across my belly.

I nodded, unable to speak. I watched him through lowered lashes. He really was perfect. I could stare at him for hours.

He removed my shirt, sitting back on his heels to admire me briefly. Then he kissed the top of my pubic bone, taking his time to worship me properly by laying tender kisses all along the top of my sex. In my memories from the wedding, he had proven he was beyond talented at this. I squirmed against the bed, wanting his mouth lower. Wanting to feel his tongue slide against me, but unsure of how to ask for what I needed. Braydon didn't make me ask. He continued his descent, pushing my thighs apart and out of the way as he lowered his mouth to taste me. I drew in a sharp inhale when his tongue made contact, lazily circling my clit.

"You like that, kitten?" he whispered softly against my core.

I let out a ragged breath, whimpering from the loss of contact. "Y-yes . . ."

Chuckling softly at my response, he kissed me again. He read my body's signals, using his whole mouth, his tongue, his lips, to kiss me greedily right where I needed him. He adjusted his style to my moans, flicking his tongue ruthlessly against me, increasing his rhythm as my breathy pants increased in volume. I wasn't shy about letting him know what I liked. What I needed. With other guys, I overthought everything. I worried about my appearance, my scent, if my apartment was clean, if I'd shaved. I wondered if he'd want to stay over and if I had breakfast food in the house to make him something in the morning that would impress him—the list went on. With Braydon, I stayed in the moment. He made me feel comfortable enough that none of the superficial bullshit mattered. It was refreshing.

His long index finger penetrated me and my back arched off the bed at the invasion. God, that felt incredible. His tongue continued its lazy strokes while his finger curled toward my inside wall and lightly rubbed. The pleasure was like nothing else. His skill was too much. My whole world came undone. I pushed my fingers into his hair and tugged him closer, shamelessly rocking my hips as I came.

Dizzy and disoriented, I became aware of Braydon pulling the comforter up around me and tucking me into bed. "Good night, gorgeous. Get some sleep."

Once again he didn't expect anything in return. I would have felt bad if I could have moved just then. But I wouldn't have been much use to him in that moment. I was warm and sleepy and incredibly relaxed, so I just nodded.

He pressed a soft kiss to my mouth. "Do you need to lock up behind me?"

"Yes, please." Oops. I'd forgotten about that. I crawled from the bed and accepted his proffered hand, letting him guide me to the front door.

"Everything okay, kitten?"

"Yes, tonight was . . . interesting."

He smiled his crooked grin that made my heart kick up a notch. "Interesting good or interesting bad?"

"Good, I think."

He lifted my hand to his mouth and kissed the tops of my fingers, his eyes on mine. "It will be. I promise." His words sent a rush through me. "Night. Sleep well."

"Night," I whispered back.

The door closed behind him and I slid to the floor in a boneless heap.

Fuck. I was already in over my head.

4

I should've just cut my losses but I knew I wouldn't. Spending time with Braydon made me feel alive and desirable in a way I hadn't felt before. I wasn't ready to give that up. Besides, part of me felt a little guilty that both times we'd hooked up had been solely about me. I hadn't returned the favor and I was dying with curiosity to know if the chemistry we had would translate into mind-blowing sex. I wanted to touch and explore the body I'd admired from afar since the moment I'd met him.

So when he texted me later that week, it was with shaky fingers that I pondered what to write back.

Braydon: Hey gorgeous. How's your day?

Me: Hey. It's fine. It's been a long day and I could use a massage.

Braydon: Let me come over tonight and I'll give you a gentle massage from the inside out. ;)

This was how it started. Naughty texts. Flirty comments.

My heart squeezed tightly in my chest. There was no denying I wanted to see him tonight. To see his big smile light up his face and watch his playful eyes dance on mine. I wanted to poke fun at him and hear him chuckle. I just liked being near him.

I still hadn't responded when he sent another text.

Braydon: Shall I bring dinner again?

Me: Sure. I'm craving Italian.

Braydon: One extra-large Italian sausage cumming right up. See you at 7.

I laughed out loud and stuffed my phone back in my purse. Tonight should be interesting.

When Braydon arrived promptly at seven, I was wrestling a cork from a bottle of wine in the kitchen. I needed some liquid courage tonight. When the buzzer sounded from the intercom on my wall, I abandoned the wine to buzz him in. A few moments later, I pulled open the front door to discover a deliciously polished Braydon. Gone were his beat-up Converse sneakers and his vintage tees. He was dressed in a button-down shirt and dark gray slacks, his hair neatly combed and ready to be tugged on. I held my breath as I drank him in and his lips smirked.

"Hiya, kitten."

"Come in." I pushed open the door and he followed me inside. I headed back to the kitchen to finish fighting with the wine bottle. Braydon chuckled at me and promptly removed it from my hands, easily finishing the job and pouring each of us a glass.

We sipped our wine while Braydon unloaded the cartons of food he'd brought. Fettuccine Alfredo with chicken, rosemary Parmesan breadsticks, spaghetti carbonara, and antipasto salad. Once again he'd brought more than enough food for just us. I could get used to eating delicious leftovers from our takeout dinners. I had just finished the Thai.

The aroma was heavenly as he dished up hearty servings into the bowls I provided. "This smells great. Where'd you get it?"

"Giovanni's. It's a hole in the wall, but the food is fantastic." He twirled a forkful of pasta and held it up, intending to feed me the bite. "Open," he commanded.

I obeyed, accepting a mouthful of spaghetti. My eyes slipped closed, savoring the subtle flavors of homemade pasta, black pepper, and crisp bacon. It was delicious. And I liked that he fed me. I accepted another bite while Braydon's eyes watched my mouth. The temperature in my apartment seemed to ratchet up in an instant. I licked my bottom lip and chewed slowly, swallowing the bite of food while his breathing grew shallow.

"Everything okay?" he asked, his voice low and commanding.

I nodded slowly. It was as if he could tell when I was retreating into my head to overthink everything and knew when to distract me to keep me from questioning things between us.

"Good. Let's eat." We sat down at the table that I used so rarely, though we'd used it two times together this week already. We even had our own spots at the table. A little routine was developing.

"You're dressed up," I noticed, taking him in.

"I had casting calls today. Dress to impress."

I nodded. Made sense.

"How was your day?" he asked, taking a bite of his dinner.

"Good, actually. I've been giving our arrangement more thought, too."

"Oh yeah?"

"Yes."

"Tell me."

"Well, you want to be penis pals . . ."

His brow creased as he squinted at me. "Not exactly. I hope you don't have a penis, kitten."

I frowned at him. "Fine then. You want to be best friends with my vagina."

His head cocked to the side and a slow smile overtook his mouth. "I thought I already was."

I rolled my eyes. "Unfortunately, you do seem to be." My eyes dropped to my plate and I twirled strands of pasta onto my fork. I didn't know how to ask about our arrangement and stared down at my food, poking at the lump of pasta, hoping he'd pick up the conversation where I'd dropped it. Only he didn't.

"Eat up." Braydon grinned, his dimple peeking at me. "You'll need your energy."

Yes, sir. "So bossy." I shook my head.

We kept up a casual conversation through dinner, enjoying good food, pleasant company, and the easy conversation that flowed so well between us. But I didn't find the courage to bring up our arrangement again. And Braydon didn't push it. This was all so new to me. I was hoping he'd take the lead, but so far he seemed content to discuss my job, local sports teams—anything but why he was here.

Soon, we were both full and Braydon was helping me pack up the leftovers. I wanted to inquire about his diet requirements for his job, but I didn't want him to stop feeding me like this. I was getting spoiled already and I liked it.

I lingered in the kitchen, wiping a nonexistent spot on the counter.

"Hey." His hand curled around my shoulder pulled me from my thoughts. "Whatcha thinking about?"

"Nothing," I lied. *Everything. This. Us. How much better homemade pasta is than boxed. Why your dimple makes me weak in the knees.*

"Come sit down. Finish your wine." He refilled my glass, pouring a healthy amount.

"Trying to get me drunk?" I smiled.

"Will that work?"

I shook my head slowly. "Nope."

"I know." His thumb traced the crease between my brows. "You're too smart for that." His thumb stroked the spot again before he lowered his hand. "It's something I like about you. But sometimes you've got to stop thinking so hard and just feel. See where things take you."

I brought my glass to my lips and took a fortifying swallow. He was right. I wanted to feel alive. To have a naughty little escapade. My life was so mapped out and organized, just him being here threw off my routine in a good way. Normally I'd be in pajamas, flipping mindlessly through the channels and feeling sorry for myself. Or worse, torturing myself by trolling the Internet, looking at my friends' pages on social media and seeing engagement rings and baby bumps.

"There, that's better." He could read me way too well. It was like he could see the exact moment my brain stopped fighting my body and I mentally gave in. "Don't be scared. I won't bite." He narrowed his eyes. "Actually I might. But you'll like it."

Pressing his fingertips into my lower back, he guided me to the living room and we settled on the sofa. I pulled my legs up and hugged my knees, suddenly feeling contemplative. How was it that this man I'd known only a short time could read me better than anyone?

Braydon watched me carefully, moving the throw pillow between us to the floor, as if needing to remove any and all physical barriers between us. "Tell me something, kitten, because I won't pressure you into this. I won't make you do something you don't want. How sure are you about this arrangement I've proposed?"

No thinking, Ellie. Feeling only. "No one has ever made me come like you have," I admitted softly. *Holy crap! I can't believe I just said that.*

"I'm just getting started, baby. I can't wait to show you all the things I can do to your body."

Sucking in a soft inhale, I unconsciously leaned closer, letting him draw me into his orbit. He pressed forward and touched his lips softly to mine, lingering there, not rushing me, and in turn making me crave him even more. His breath mingled with mine, the soft warmth teasing me, promising a raw heat between us, if only I'd give in. Give up control. I brought my hands up and pushed them into his hair, rumpling it into a sexy disarray, just like I'd wanted to do when I'd opened the door earlier tonight and seen it styled neatly. I clutched his dark locks between my fingers and forced him closer, kissing his full mouth like I wanted to, giving in to my body.

He groaned into my mouth, matching the intensity of my kiss and massaging my tongue with his. He tasted of wine. It was intoxicating. He pulled my hand into his lap and pressed it to the erection pushing against his zipper. "See what you do to me. You get me so worked up just by being near me." My hand curled around him and I squeezed, enjoying the soft way his breath pushed past his parted lips. Suddenly rising from the couch, Braydon found my hand and tugged me up. "Take me to your bedroom."

I nodded and guided him down the hall.

We fell back onto my bed, which I'd made that morning in anticipation of our date—er, *arrangement*. He pushed my thighs apart with his knee, caged me in with his firm body, and kissed my neck, trailing rough kisses and small nips. It felt forbidden and intoxicating. He was marking my flesh, and I wanted to wear the evidence of this erotic encounter tomorrow. I couldn't resist rocking my hips and pushing myself onto his thigh, needing contact against my swollen, achy center. Lifting himself off me just briefly, Braydon unbuttoned and unzipped my pants and slid them, along with my panties, down my legs before I even knew what was happening. But we both knew I wasn't about to stop him. I was whimpering with need and squirming already.

I sat up and pulled my T-shirt over my head then reached behind me to unclasp my bra. I wanted to be bold just then. To undress for him. Not some quick and dirty fuck. I wanted to take my time. Get the full experience, in case this was it—all I would get from him.

Braydon watched in wonder as I let my bra drop away from my shoulders, but at the last possible second I brought my hands up to cover my naked breasts. Maybe I wasn't so brave after all.

"No." He shook his hand, his fingers circling my wrists. "I want to see all of you. Don't hide from me."

My heart pounded steadily and I let him pull my hands away, baring myself to him fully. His eyes lingered on mine just a moment before sliding down my chest.

He swallowed roughly. "Perfect. Gorgeous tits. Never hide these." His head lowered and without warning he began sucking on my breast, his tongue circling my nipple, his teeth lightly grazing the peak, drawing it into a hardened bud. Damn, that felt incredible. He wasn't shy about using his teeth. And he did so expertly, eliciting pleasure from my body in ways I'd never even imagined. I slipped my fingers into his hair again and pressed my breasts forward with a low moan. Sparks of primal need coursed through my system. He captured my wrists, pinning them at my sides. Oops. Maybe I'd been pulling his hair a little too hard.

"Sorry," I murmured.

His mouth pulled suddenly from my breast. "I love when you play with my hair. I just want you focused on feeling the sensations I give you rather than touching me."

Oh. He was too thoughtful. Too in tune with my body. It sent a shudder through me.

He continued licking and nipping at my breasts, the warm pad of his tongue sending pulses of pleasure through me. He was right; the sensations were stronger when I wasn't preoccupied with touching him. I closed my eyes and just let myself feel. He slowly moved lower, planting soft kisses against my rib cage, my belly, as he made his way south. My pulse spiked in anticipation, already imagining his skilled tongue against me. But rather than obliging me with his mouth at my core, he positioned himself lower on the bed, between my parted legs, and observed me writhing for him with a tug pulling his mouth upward. I hated how he alone could turn me into a wanton creature, so ready to dive off the deep end with him. I reached for him, wanting to pull him closer, and my fists twisted in the folds of his shirt.

He had far too many clothes on. I wanted to see him, to feel his warm skin, to breathe him in. I began tugging at his clothing. "Your shirt."

He looked down.

"Take it off," I said breathily.

"Anything for you." He unbuttoned just the first few buttons then pulled it over his head.

"Your pants, too," I begged.

He made quick work of his belt and then pushed his pants down his hips in one quick movement, discarding them beside the bed. I couldn't help but steal a peek. My gaze wandered down the length of his lean torso, taking him in. He was masculine. Beautiful. Toned and solid from his broad chest to his chiseled abs to his . . . *wait*. He dropped his boxer briefs to the floor and looked up at me. I couldn't help my eyes from widening, and then squeezing closed. *Holy shit!*

"Kitten?" My eyes flew open and then I looked down at him again, shifting on the bed uncomfortably. He followed my gaze downward and his mouth pulled up in a lazy grin. "What's wrong?" He looked down at himself and then back up at me. "You don't like my body?"

I shook my head in disbelief. "Your body is insane; you know that. It's just, well . . . *that*"—I looked down again—"is . . . um, bigger than I was expecting."

His chest ballooned out and his smile broke wider. "I won't hurt you. I promise." He bent forward and pressed a kiss to my forehead. The gesture was sweet. Almost too much so. It implied a closeness between us that shouldn't have been present. This was just sex, yet it felt like more.

"Just tell me what you can handle," he whispered, rubbing his nose along my jaw. "Okay, miss?"

I nodded, my mouth curling up in a smile. Feeling braver, I attempted another look at his member. A glint of silver caught my eye. *What the?* "What's that?" I felt like a kid at the zoo, pointing and staring. But I couldn't help myself. I'd never seen something like that in real life.

"It's a piercing. You'll like it, I promise." His hand captured his steely length and he stroked himself slowly while I watched, utterly mesmerized, his hand gliding up and down over the head and the silver ball of his piercing. "You ready for me, kitten?" His hand slid along his thick shaft. He was long and straight. Deliciously so. I couldn't wait to slide my mouth around him, to flick my tongue across his naughty piercing. But I didn't get that chance.

Positioning himself lower on the bed, Braydon pushed my legs apart. "Open for me," he whispered, and my body obeyed, legs sliding wider to accommodate him. He pressed a single finger inside me, slowly, achingly slowly, parting me and making my back arch up off the bed. His finger penetrated me in a steady rhythm, curling up just slightly to massage my inner wall. He added a second finger, fucking me with his hand, and I moaned out, taken back by how incredible he made everything feel. Everything was about me. He was solely focused on my pleasure.

His cock pressed against my thigh as he shifted closer. He was rock hard, warm, and ready. The hint of hard metal warmed to body temperature tempted me beyond belief. What would he feel like inside? I twisted and writhed as he fucked me with his fingers. My inner muscles clenched around his fingers as I came. Pleasure blinded me momentarily as white spots danced in my vision.

Slowly opening my eyes, I found him watching me. I'd never had an orgasm so fast. Holy shit, this man was talented. Was that my G-spot? I thought that was a mythical creature, like a unicorn or a Sasquatch.

He crawled up my body, kissing my stomach, my chest, my neck, until his lips found mine. He kissed me fiercely, my only clue that he was as desperate for me as I was for him. Blood pounded in my ears as my body took control. He was an itch I desperately wanted to scratch, a need so deep I felt it in my core. My heart pounded erratically and my lungs screamed for oxygen, but stopping wasn't an option. I'd never felt anything so intense. Tongues stroked and mingled as we fought to get closer. Braydon pulled away, his mouth moving to my throat where I felt the pinch of his teeth graze my skin.

I squirmed against the mattress, boneless and content. The deep ache within me was momentarily soothed, but still I wanted more. "I want to come again," I murmured.

"I know you do." He reached for a condom packet he'd inconspicuously placed on the bedside table. When had he done that? The package was gold and I recognized the brand. *Magnum.* "Roll over," he commanded with a firm gentleness to his voice.

I watched as he tore open the packet with his teeth and began to unroll it onto himself before I obeyed, rolling over onto my stomach. Cool air rushed over my skin, my backside exposed as I waited.

Lying flat on my stomach, I felt him move on top of me, his thighs on either side of mine. His fingertips lightly trailed down my spine, softly tickling and caressing me. I craved him and whimpered at his lightest touch. Anticipating the moment he'd take me, I squirmed, holding my breath for the invasion.

He positioned himself against me and pressed forward. The blunt head of him nudged against me, seeking entrance. "Relax your body. Breathe for me. You're too tense."

I closed my eyes and focused on relaxing and accepting his length. He disappeared inch by inch, sliding slowly inside me from behind, keeping his grip firmly on my hips until his fingers bit into the skin. The too-full sensations gave way to raw pleasure and I pressed back against him, taking him in.

He kept his pace slow and careful as I got used to him moving behind me, sliding out and pushing in again incrementally. It'd been a while since I'd had a lover, and he felt incredible. The piercing provided a bit of extra friction in just the right spot, and I whimpered out loud. Unable to resist working my hips against him, I was soon restless and moaning into the bed beneath me, grasping the sheets in my palms.

I wanted to see him, to kiss him, to watch his eyes as he took me. "I want to fuck you," I moaned.

He leaned closer, his lips brushing the shell of my ear. "You want to ride me?"

"Yeah . . ." I groaned, happily pushing my bottom up to

meet his hips. Suddenly he was retreating and helping me up. Positioning himself, he propped his back against the headboard, and I climbed onto his lap. His hands cupped my jaw and we kissed deeply, just like I'd been craving. "Let me," I groaned, needing him to fill me up once again. I aligned his length to my entrance and slowly lowered myself down. Gasping at the invasion, I pressed my palms flat against his chiseled abs and rotated my hips lightly, adjusting to the feel of him. *Whoa.* It was deep like this.

His palms cupped my naked breasts and he pinched my nipples, pulling slightly. "Ahhh . . ." I groaned. "Gentle . . ." I reminded him.

"I can be gentle with you . . ." he murmured, lightly trailing featherlight fingertips across my skin. He took my hands and moved them to his throat. "But you can be rough with me, kitten. Choke me if you want." His eyes were smiling, but his tone was sincere. I wasn't much into kink, but the idea that this man could open me up to a new world excited me.

I circled my hands around his throat without applying any pressure and leaned down to kiss him again. His breath left his lips in a rush, spurring me on. Rubbing my sensitive nipples against his chest, I circled my hips slowly, drawing in more of his length.

Once he was buried inside me, his hands clutched my waist, his fingers nipping into the skin. "Ah, shit." His eyes dropped closed and a look of complete bliss overtook his features. "Your pussy feels so good."

"Don't they all feel the same?" I wasn't sure how many girls he'd been with, but surely the number was up there.

"No." His tone was firm.

"How does it feel?" I seriously wanted to know. I knew what this felt like on my end—an intense, breath-stealing fullness as he pushed into me—but I had no clue what it felt like for him.

"Are you going to talk the whole time?" His mouth quirked up in a smile.

"Tell me," I demanded.

He let out a deep groan as I lifted and lowered slowly. "You feel warm and wet, nice and tight. Perfect." Gripping my hips, he pushed upward suddenly, his long cock bumping against my cervix. *Gah! He was* so *big.* My movements turned frenzied as I started to ride him again. His hands caught my hips, lifting me against him. All too soon, he flipped me so that I was lying on my back and he was on top once again. At least this time I could see him. He kissed me softly and thrust forward.

Holy God. I flinched involuntarily. "You're too big."

"Am I hurting you? I'm trying to be careful." His voice went all whispery soft and concerned. It was sweet.

"You're too rough."

"I'm being gentle," he whispered. "But I'm not going to stop biting your clavicle." His teeth grazed the tender skin again, making me shiver. He pushed into me, his entire length owning me, making my back arch off the bed.

"Not so deep." I curled my hand around the base of him,

my hand blocking his last few inches from entering me. There, that was better. "Do you normally have this problem with girls?"

"Sometimes," he admitted. *Holy fuck, of course he did. This was ridiculous.* "But I wouldn't call it a problem. You'll see once you get accustomed."

Maybe it was the piercing, but something about him was causing my entire body to shiver and blossom in awesomeness. Wait, was that even a word? I didn't care. I was going to come. Again. I wrapped my legs around his back and let him pound into me. The pleasure-pain combo heated my skin and made me whimper. I buried my face against his neck as I came, my entire world exploding in brilliant white light. He held me tight, wrapping both arms around me.

Coming down from my release, I tried the biting thing he seemed to be so fond of. I nibbled his jaw, his throat, and felt his blood pumping there, sure and strong. It was kind of fun, and Braydon's groan when my teeth made contact with his neck was a plus. He still hadn't finished, despite the several orgasms I'd already had.

"You're too big," I groaned again. "Let me give you a hand job instead." I needed to climb off this ride. It was too much. Far too intense for me to handle.

He chuckled against my throat. "I can't have a hand job after this. Your pussy feels so fucking good," he groaned. He kept the next few thrusts shallow and whispered against my skin, "I'm going to come."

Fuck, thank God.

He pressed his lips to my throat, suppressing his groans as he spilled himself inside me.

Afterward, I curled into a ball and pulled my knees to my chest, my heart thumping wildly. What in the world was that? Braydon, who annoyed me to no end, was the best lover I'd ever had.

"Are you okay?" his voice had gone all soft and concerned again.

"Oh, you mean other than having a punctured ovary? I'm fabulous." I could seriously use some pain reliever right about now. I considered sending him into the kitchen for a dose of medicine, but decided against it. I didn't want to stroke his ego any more than I already had.

He chuckled under his breath and bent down to kiss my forehead. "I'm not that big, kitten. You're just little."

I waggled my finger at his protruding member. "Well that's not happening again." Shit, at this rate I'd need to call in sick to work tomorrow. I doubted I could walk right now. I'd be bowlegged at the very least. I peeked one eye open and watched him yank off the condom with a snap. *Ouch.* That just looked painful. He treaded into the bathroom, the soles of his bare feet padding against the tiled floor. What little light there was in the room provided a view of his toned backside. Mmm. Maybe there'd be a repeat after all, once I was all healed up. At the very least, I'd let him do that G-spot thingy to me again. That was fine by me. Seriously, what was that?

The bathroom door closed behind him and I heard the water running. I lay there, watching the light filtering through the crack at the bottom of the door, wondering if he'd dress and leave when he emerged or if he'd want to stay the night. The thought of him leaving just now, after such an intense experience, was depressing. I had no clue where these feelings were coming from, but cuddling sounded amazing right about now. Feeling his strong arms around me . . . drifting off to sleep with his firm body beside mine . . . sounded like bliss. Maybe I was just starved for male attention. This was Braydon, after all. Male model and man-whore, whom I had fought to steer clear of, initially. Yet, he'd been nothing but a gentleman so far, using a condom without me having to request it, ensuring I got off first, which sadly was more than I could say for most guys, and adjusting his style when I said it was too rough. He'd already exceeded my low expectations for what a one-night stand was supposed to be.

The bathroom door opened and the light flipped off. Braydon crossed the room to the bed and climbed in beside me. My lips curled up in a smile. I liked that there was no question, no discussion. He was sleeping over.

In my apartment.

With me.

I relaxed into the mattress and let out a breath I didn't know I was holding. Maybe this arrangement would be okay after all.

He pulled the fluffy down comforter up around us and curled both arms around me, burying his face against my neck. "That was amazing, gorgeous," he said, his warm breath whispering across my neck.

"Mmm," I returned, unable to form words just yet.

"You feel perfect." He tugged me to him, closing all distance between us. Surprisingly, it was comfortable. I wasn't the best cuddler, and considering he and I had never even come close to sharing a bed, I shouldn't have been so at ease. Yet, I was. Totally and completely. Without overanalyzing every little thing, I relaxed into his embrace, just enjoying the moment.

Nature called, though, and all too soon I was crawling out of bed to use the bathroom and get ready to sleep. My reflection in the mirror was unexpected. My cheeks were flushed, my hair was a mess, but mostly I just looked happy. *Huh.*

"Are you brushing your teeth in there?" Braydon called. The sound of running water must have given me away.

"Yes," I said around a garbled mouthful of bubbles.

"I'm so jealous right now," he admitted.

"You can too if you want."

"Use your toothbrush?" he asked.

"Why not?" His mouth had been on my most private of parts. Cooties were null and void at this point.

Braydon remained in my bed, though, looking rather comfortable I might add. He somehow knew which side was mine and positioned himself on the opposite one. When I crawled back in beside him, he wrapped me in his arms and whispered goodnight. I settled into his broad, warm body, closed my eyes, and promptly fell into a deep and restful sleep.

5

A loud blasting sound startled me awake. *What the . . . ?*

I scrambled from bed, frantically searching for the source of the sound. It was like a damn fire alarm going off. Braydon rolled over and grabbed his cell phone from the bedside table, silencing it with a grunt and then rolling back over and shutting his eyes.

My heart was pounding against my ribs and my fists were tightly balled at my sides. I was coiled as tight as a damn wire. "What the fuck was that?"

One hazy blue eye opened. "Sorry. I can't hear my alarm unless it's loud."

"Loud? Sweetie, I thought Armageddon was here."

He opened his eyes, slowly blinking at me, and his mouth turned up just a fraction. "Get your sweet ass over here, girl."

I sighed dramatically like it was some great hardship but crawled back in beside him, letting him spoon his large frame around me.

"Next time I'll turn the volume down so that it wakes you up but doesn't freak you out. Then you can wake me up."

"Next time, huh?" I grinned.

"Yes. And if you're taking requests, I prefer to be woken up with your mouth on my dick."

"Ha," I snorted. "You're quite demanding. That's not happening."

His hand moved under my tank top and splayed flat against my belly. His touch made my stomach jump. "Are you feeling okay?" he murmured, pressing his nose into my hair.

"A little sore," I admitted.

He planted a tender kiss to the back of my neck. He could be so sweet and tender at times and so intensely passionate at others. My mind flashed to our lovemaking last night . . . when he'd bitten and marked me and suggested I choke him. A shiver raced up my spine.

Not missing a thing, his hands smoothed over my back. "Goose bumps. Are you cold?"

I merely nodded and burrowed deeper into his embrace. He was warm and firm and smelled so good. I didn't want to move. But remembering what'd woken us in the first place, I rolled to face him. "Do you have somewhere to be this morning?"

He nodded, pushing my messy hair back from my face. "Yes. I have a charity thing."

"Oh."

"My agent arranged for me to help out with some projects at a veterans' home today."

"Are you handy?" I asked. It seemed at odds with his profession.

"With a hammer and nails and a bucket of paint, sure. I don't think they'll have me do anything too complex." He stretched and sat up in bed. "I'm sorry I have to run. Last night was . . ." He shook his head like he couldn't keep the smile from overtaking his face. "Pretty fucking awesome."

Heat rose in my cheeks as I watched him move across the room, gathering articles of clothing and dressing as the warm morning sunlight streamed in through my bedroom window. He bent to kiss my forehead and moments later he was gone. The soft sound of my front door closing and the ache deep in my womb were the only evidence he'd been here at all. I rolled over in bed, hugged his still-warm pillow to my chest, and inhaled. His scent lingered. The perfect mixture of natural masculine musk, spicy cologne, and soap. I was warm and still sleepy and let myself drift back off for a few hours.

When I woke for the second time that morning, the tiny ache in my womb reminded me of him. Of where he'd been. Of how he'd claimed me so completely. It was both too much and not enough at the same time. Quieting the silly thoughts running through my head, I stumbled from bed to start my Saturday.

I made coffee alone in my silent kitchen. I missed Emmy. I missed Braydon's easy company. I hated how lonely I felt. How empty my apartment seemed. I knew I should do something with myself, go for a run, clean my apartment. But instead, I ran a warm bath and sunk inside with a mug of steaming coffee and a gossip magazine. Something mindless to flip through.

Of course I hadn't counted on spotting Braydon's photo in an advertisement for men's cologne. I stopped on that page and stared at it for far too long, even lifting up the flap of paper to smell the intoxicating scent. It wasn't the cologne he wore, but the scent was still delicious. I lay there soaking in the warm water, letting the spicy masculine scent drift over my senses and lull me into a state of deep relaxation, with thoughts of Braydon swirling in my brain.

I wondered if he'd given me a second thought once he'd left, or if he was used to compartmentalizing his one-night stands until the urge for the next hookup struck him. I didn't want to feel insecure, but a part of me couldn't help but dwell on it.

I breathed in a slow, measured breath. I needed to clear my head of all this Braydon Kincaid nonsense. He was a god-damn supermodel. I was a microbiologist who was too busy to take care of my split ends and didn't mind having cellulite on my ass. Yes, we had great chemistry, but that was it. He wasn't my happily ever after. Hell, he wasn't even boyfriend material. He was a notorious playboy and his work made a real relationship difficult—two things that gave Emmy trouble when she first started dating Ben. And he was very clear about what he wanted: to fuck me. So why was I allowing myself to get so worked up over him?

As much as I tried to deny it, I knew I wanted him. But I couldn't sit around waiting around for him until he decided to call me again. I wouldn't. I needed to man up. I rose from the bath, toweled off, and decided I'd go on my jog after all.

6

I couldn't take it anymore. I broke down and upgraded my phone to an international calling plan just so I could call Emmy. I missed her terribly and needed to hear her sweet voice. That little southern accent made everything better. I needed a pep talk. I needed my bestie.

She told me they were having a wonderful time and were getting ready to come home soon, though they'd considered just looking for properties in Tahiti and staying there permanently.

"What's going on with you? Had any dates lately?" she asked.

"No," I lied. "Nothing at all."

"Have you seen Braydon again?"

"That was a one-time thing." I had no clue why I was lying to my best friend, but something about my agreement with Braydon made me feel dirty. He was my little secret. "Can you come home early?" I begged, selfishly.

Emmy laughed. "Three more days till we're reunited, babe. You want to do lunch when I get home? Maybe get pedicures?"

"Duh. Call me the second you land. I'm coming straight over. And I can't be held responsible for dry-humping your leg like an overexcited lapdog when I see you."

She laughed and we ended the call that was probably costing me a fortune per minute. But the sad, lonely feeling came back the moment I said good-bye.

How had it come to this? I felt pathetic. And I was sleeping with someone without any hope of commitment? Geez. How the mighty had fallen.

Maybe I was being too hard on myself. Hadn't I encouraged Emmy to just go for it when she'd been so torn over Ben? Perhaps this arrangement with Braydon was exactly what I needed. I was too in my damn head all the time. I worked in a demanding field, I lived alone, and I rarely made time for fun. I couldn't remember the last time I'd felt that giddy butterfly feeling that I'd felt when Braydon and I had made love. *Shit.* I mean had sex. Fucked. That was definitely not making love. If I was going to survive this arrangement, I needed to keep my head in the game. This was about one megahot model with a huge, pierced schlong. Period. I could do this. I just needed to man up.

Grabbing life by the balls, I pulled up Braydon's number and began a new text, pacing the room while I typed.

Me: Heyyy, it's me. Wanna come over and play?

Two seconds later my phone pinged. What a lovely little

sound. I was thankful he didn't make me wait. The sting of rejection would have been too much.

Braydon: You sure you can handle me this time? ;)

Me: Guess we'll find out.

Braydon: Guess we will.

A few hours later, Braydon arrived. He grabbed a beer from my fridge and plopped down on my couch, kicking his feet up on the leather trunk, looking relaxed and happy.

"Make yourself comfortable," I said with a smirk, falling into the chair beside him.

"Oh, I will." He grinned at me. The one where his mouth pulled up crookedly and showed off his dimple. Sweet baby Jesus. I clamped my thighs together while he brought the bottle to his lips for another swig, seemingly unaware of the sexual yearnings he so easily produced within my body.

"Have you had dinner?" he asked.

"No," I admitted. Food hadn't really been on my mind when inviting him here.

"I'm starving. You want to eat?"

"Sure. Let me grab my purse." I hopped up from the chair.

"Nah. We'll stay in, get something delivered," he said, crossing his feet at the ankles and relaxing back into the sofa.

"Oh. Sure. That works." I couldn't help but notice his reluctance to go out. Did he not want to be seen in public with me? I was certain I was being irrational, but something about the situation tugged at the back corner of my mind. He was hungry and it was easier to order in, I told myself. Except that

I had a great deli just down the street from my building that he surely passed by every time he came to my apartment. It'd be quick and easy to just go down there. Maybe there was something about our arrangement that he wanted to keep hidden. I decided to test my theory.

"You don't always have to come here, I can go to your place sometimes, too," I offered.

"Nah, that's okay."

"I'd like to. I mean, I don't even know where you live."

The set of his jaw turned serious. "I don't really have people over."

"Braydon, I don't care if your place is a mess."

"No, it's nothing like that. I'm just sort of private about my personal space."

I blew out a frustrated breath. He'd been inside me, yet I couldn't see his apartment? God, men were confusing.

Pushing away the thoughts, I wandered into the kitchen and grabbed the stack of takeout menus from my cupboard. "What are you in the mood for?" I asked, sitting next to him on the couch and dumping the papers into his lap.

"Let's order from Pow Thai Café. I'm craving their lemongrass shrimp."

"Poo Poo Café? Ew. No thanks."

He chuckled. "Poo Poo?"

"Yeah, that place makes you poop."

His mouth twitched in a smile. "Newsflash, Ellie. All food makes you poop."

"Yes, but I'd rather not take a direct laxative right now. Seriously, that place and my stomach do not mix."

He shook his head at me, still smirking. "That was probably more information than I needed, but thanks for sharing. You pick the place then."

"The Eat Shop. And they deliver, too, since you're so anti going out."

His mouth pulled down in a frown. "Fine. Get me whatever you recommend."

I ordered couscous salad and grilled salmon while Braydon continued quietly sitting on my couch, sipping his beer and watching me. This arrangement between us confused me. I had figured the majority of the time we'd spend together would be between the sheets. But this felt like more than just sex. This was different. Comfortably ordering delivery together, chatting casually, sipping beers on my couch . . . It felt like more.

When our food arrived, we served ourselves then settled back onto the couch. He talked between bites of salmon and couscous and I listened, genuinely interested in learning more about him. He told me about his many passions—working out, good food, handcrafted beers, and sex. I almost choked when I heard that last one.

"Care to tell me why you're so antimen?" Braydon asked, taking a bite of his salmon.

"Let's see . . . my last boyfriend had a habit of filming the girls he slept with. He had over twenty videos of girls, and I was rumored to be one of them." I poked at the salad on my plate.

"Shit." His eyebrows shot up. "But you weren't?"

"No, thank God. Then there was the guy who I thought was a car salesman but turned out to be just a car thief instead." I waited for his judgment but none came. "Basically, my dating experiences the last few years have taught me one thing—that men are not to be trusted."

"I can't argue with any of that, so I won't try. But I'm sorry you had to go through that."

"Yeah, thanks." I picked at the hem of my shirt, plucking imaginary lint from it. "It was quite a string of bad luck. I was starting to think it was me."

His expression turned serious, his eyes darkening. "It's not you. Trust me."

"How can you be so sure?"

"You're lovely. Quite a catch, kitten." His words were too kind. Too sweet, considering the kind of arrangement we had. Being sweet to me only deepened my feelings for him. Which wasn't good. He'd been very clear about our relationship. Or lack thereof. I needed to remember that.

"What about you? No past relationships? Any ex-girl-friends I should be aware of?"

His expression darkened further and he set down his plate on the ottoman in front of us. "Why do you ask?"

"No reason. I just noticed in your pictures online that you never have a girl with you. There was even one blog claiming you were gay."

"I like pussy way too much to be gay. I guess you're right, though, I do tend to fly solo, mostly. I don't typically bring the girls I'm seeing to events with me."

I wasn't talking about events. I never expected to be on his arm walking the red carpet. I was referring to simple things like meeting for breakfast or going to the movies, but I merely nodded. Something told me not to push him on this. I swallowed a lump of unease in my throat. He was so fun and easygoing one minute and then so guarded and closed off the next.

Braydon Kincaid, my own little Rubik's Cube to solve.

After dinner we cuddled together on the couch, Braydon with his legs resting on the ottoman and me with my feet curled under me while I leaned against his shoulder.

"Sooo . . . our arrangement . . . what happens when Ben and Emmy get home?" I asked.

"What about them? What you and I have is no one's business but our own."

I nodded, my heart silently pinching in my chest. After several minutes of silence, his eyes slowly raked over me, making me shiver. The longer he watched me, the further away thoughts of refusing him drifted. "Do you have any idea how fucking sexy you look right now?" he asked.

I looked down at my yoga pants and comfy T-shirt, my brain struggling to comprehend if he was kidding or being serious.

"Most girls want to impress me with their designer clothes, lingerie, accessories, makeup . . ." He leaned closer.

"No one's ever like this with me, you know? I like that you're confident enough to just be you."

His words meant a lot to me, only I had no idea how to react to them. Were we good buddies? Something more? "Who else would I be?" I joked.

The seriousness of the mood fell away as Braydon let out a chuckle. He set down his beer and turned to me with a playful smile. "Sooo . . ." he rubbed his hands together. "What shall we do to entertain ourselves?"

I faked a yawn and stretched my arms over my head. "I'm exhausted. You're welcome to stay and entertain yourself, though. There's lube in my nightstand drawer if you need it."

He let out a snort and tackled me on the couch. "Get over here." He pressed me to the sofa, careful not to crush me under his weight but making sure I felt his firm body covering mine. "Why would I take care of myself when you have two perfectly functioning hands?" He traced a single fingertip over my lips. "And this pretty mouth I'd like to fuck."

My insides went molten, sending a jab of lust through me. "You're pretty confident there, mister."

"I always get what I want."

"And what do you want?" I challenged, finding that spark within myself once again as we bantered.

"To lay you down in your bed and make you come."

His words melted me while bringing up all of my fears, despite the fact that I was trying to man up here. "After all of my dating mishaps, I don't trust myself to make the right decisions about men."

"Then trust your body." He curled a strong hand around my wrist, drawing me closer. "What does it tell you?"

My pulse spiked, my breathing became labored, and my nipples hardened into points. Instead of making me feel cheap and used, Braydon made me feel vital and cherished. He could read my body so well, he seemed to know my hidden desires without me needing to voice them, but I realized I didn't know much of what he desired.

"What do you like?" I murmured.

"I like an aggressive girl who goes after what she wants, when she wants it."

Normally I was that way. But not so much with him. I wasn't sure why. Maybe because he was so confident and sure that my body chose to submit to him rather than compete for control. I wanted to hand him the reins and let him take over. And I hadn't felt that way about a man, well . . . ever. I pushed him off me and Braydon frowned slightly as he sat up. But when I took his hand and tugged him to my bedroom, his sexy, playful smile was back in full force and my insides did a little flip-flop.

We settled on the bed and Braydon pulled me close, kissing my neck and the ticklish spot behind my ear. I let out a soft moan. "You're so sexual," he breathed against my skin.

"I'm sorry?"

His mouth lifted in a smile as he chuckled softly. "It's one of the things I love about you."

Hearing Braydon mention the word *love* in relation to me wasn't healthy. I had to reel my brain in from barraging me with images of us dashing off into the sunset, me in a white poufy dress. "What is?" I asked.

"You're such a firecracker. So sassy, intelligent, and confident. You don't take any shit. But then when we're together, you turn yourself over to me fully. When I'm buried deep inside you, you submit to me completely."

I dropped my head and blushed. Oops. Maybe I was too obvious in my growing feelings for him.

"It's incredibly sexy, kitten. Trust me."

I did trust him. I trusted him with my body. I knew he'd make sure I was satisfied. I just didn't trust him with my heart. But that feeling of mistrust had practically been conditioned into me from an early age. After years of infidelity, my dad had finally left my mom for his secretary. It had shown me that I needed to pick my mate carefully. I wouldn't end up bitter and broken like my mother, thanks to an asshole disguised as Mr. Right. The jury was still out on the delicious man in front of me and I needed to play this game of cat and mouse carefully.

7

"God, you skinny bitch, you're so tan," I said enviously to Emmy. I was helping her shop for a new sofa, which was why we were currently in New Jersey, courtesy of Ben and Emmy's driver, at a megahuge furniture store.

She laughed at me and headed past the sectional sofas. "Of course I'm tan; we were on a tropical island for nearly a month. I swear, I don't know how I lost weight on our honeymoon though. I ate very well—trust me." She paused to look down critically at a bright orange couch, chewing on her lip. "We did go hiking and surfing, and we had plenty of sex." She whispered the last part.

"Sex is a great workout," I agreed. We continued roaming the rows upon rows of couches and love seats. "Any of these standing out to you?"

"What do you think about something like this?" Emmy stood back, admiring a steely gray modern-looking sofa.

It suited her and Ben's style perfectly. Simple yet classy. "I think that would look great in your place."

Her smile fell when she checked the price tag. "Never mind."

I reached down and flipped the tag over to see the price myself. "Emmy," I chastised her. "It's not that expensive. You forget you're in a different income bracket now."

She picked at her fingernails, deciding what to do. After a few moments of thinking it over, she realized I was right. It was as if she were realizing, for the first time, that her life had really changed. She was no longer a single girl in the city struggling to make ends meet. For a moment, the thought struck me with a pang of sadness. I hated the idea that Emmy and I were changing, and the possibility of us growing apart because of our differences. I vowed then and there that I wouldn't let that happen. I grabbed her hand and gave it a squeeze. "I think you should get it, sweetie."

She nodded, fixing her mouth in a smile. "Yeah, I think I will. And maybe those matching chairs." She pointed to two armchairs with a geometric pattern that contained splashes of gray and mustard yellow. They were funky and the perfect complement to the solid-colored sofa.

"Definitely," I confirmed. "And these." I grabbed a couple of fluffy pillows in a pretty deep plum shade.

Emmy smiled and followed me to the front to check out. "So what's new with you?"

My secret affair with Braydon had been at the tip of my tongue all day, and I wondered if now was the time to come clean. I summoned my courage while Emmy ordered the couch and chairs and arranged delivery. "I've been seeing someone," I finally said.

"Oh my God, who?" she demanded to know, whipping around to look at me after handing her platinum credit card—complete with her new name—to the sales clerk.

"Um . . ." I swallowed a lump in my throat. "Braydon."

"Really?" She cocked her head to the side, her eyebrows darting up her forehead. "Braydon? Like, Braydon, Braydon?"

Why was there such shock in her features and surprise in her voice? "The one and only." I stood my ground, waiting to understand her reaction. "Why?"

She signed the slip of paper and passed it back to the clerk. "Bray doesn't do relationships. Ben says he's always been more of a loner."

Hearing her nickname for him irked me. I wasn't sure why, but I frowned. I never said anything about a relationship. "Well, we're not, like, openly dating," I said, dropping my voice so the sales clerk couldn't overhear. "We sort of have an . . . arrangement."

Emmy's mouth puckered in a grimace. "What kind of arrangement?"

Shit. She was going to make me say it. *We meet up for sex at my apartment.* I accepted the shopping bag of pillows from the clerk and turned for the door. "Come on. I'll explain over lunch."

Emmy's unease was obvious as Henry, her driver, drove us to a seafood restaurant for lunch. But thankfully she respected my privacy and didn't ask any more questions in his presence. Only when we were seated with glasses of iced tea and a basket of buttery rolls did we pick up our conversation again.

"So . . ." she prompted. "I thought it was just a one-time thing at our wedding reception . . ."

I tore into the bread, needing something to distract me. "Yeah, so did I. But we've begun meeting up again."

"And . . ."

"And he's made it very clear that he isn't looking for a relationship—we're just having fun and exploring the chemistry between us."

She took a sip from her straw. "I think that's fine as long as you're on the same page, too."

Yeah, that was part of the problem. I was back and forth with our agreement. I let out a soft sigh and Emmy reached across the table and gave my hand a gentle squeeze, recognition passing between us. She knew me well enough to know that it wasn't an ideal situation. It was also similar to how her relationship with Ben had begun.

Changing the topic, we chatted about her honeymoon and placed our orders, but all the while the topic of Braydon hung heavily in the air between us.

"Have you ever been to Braydon's place?" I asked out of the blue.

She shook her head. "No, Ben's only been there a couple of times. He's pretty private."

That definitely fit with what Braydon had told me about himself. Still, I was surprised that even Ben, his best friend, had hardly been to his place. It was strange, given how open he was in other ways.

Emmy smiled softly and I stole a shrimp from her plate, trying to lighten the mood. "He really is a good guy, Ells. Just be patient with him, okay?"

I nodded, suddenly feeling irrational and overly emotional. I set the shrimp down uneaten on my plate. "Yeah. I will." I was powerless to stop this thing developing between me and him. I only wished I knew where it was headed. "Emmy?"

"Hmm?" She set down the piece of bread she was nibbling on.

"There's one thing I don't understand."

"What's that?" she asked.

"How did you know about Braydon's piercing?"

Her cheeks flamed red and her eyes dropped from mine to the bread on her plate.

"Em?"

She refused to look back up, and instead sat silently spinning the large diamond ring on her finger.

I didn't know why my question caused her to shut down. I assumed Braydon himself had let it slip, or maybe, worst-case scenario, she'd somehow caught a glimpse of him in the buff during a quick change in between runway shows.

"Ugh," Emmy groaned. "Shit. I'll tell you. Just don't freak out, okay?"

Whatever she had to say, it couldn't be *that* bad, could it? "Okay," I agreed.

"So . . . in Paris, before Ben and I started dating, we were just sort of having this intense sexual affair."

"Yes." I knew that. What did that have to do with Braydon?

"Well, I met Bray one night at an afterparty where Ben had had too much to drink and he helped me get Ben back up to our hotel room." She paused, trying to let me catch up.

"And what, you and Braydon played *I'll show you mine if you show me yours* while Ben was passed out drunk?"

"No. It's not that simple."

"Keep going," I bit out, my jaw tense.

"Are you sure you want to hear this?"

The truth was, I wasn't sure. "I think I have to."

She nodded. "Well, late that night, Fiona called Ben's phone and Ben, in his drunken state, made some comment to Bray. 'Don't tell Emmy about Fiona.' I asked him about it the following day and he admitted to me that he and Braydon had been intimate with Fiona—that they'd shared her."

Whoa. I knew that type of thing went on behind closed doors, but between my own friends? It only demonstrated how very different the world of high fashion was from my own simple life. I couldn't believe Braydon had gotten it on with that megabitch who ran one of the top modeling agencies—and Emmy's former boss. In one conversation with Emmy, I was learning more about Braydon's sexual past than I had in the time I'd spent with him. This wasn't territory we'd covered.

"And you know, I was so wrapped up in Ben and I hated his relationship with Fiona."

I nodded, fearful of where this was heading.

"I felt this strange competitiveness with her and I hated that she'd shared an experience with Ben that I hadn't. I couldn't have her one-upping me. I decided if she'd had Ben and Braydon together, then I needed to, too."

Holy shit! "Emmy . . . what are you saying?" I held my breath.

"Ben arranged the whole thing. We went out to dinner and then back to his hotel room . . ." She paused. "And . . . I went to bed with both of them."

All the air was vacuumed from my lungs and I let out a gasp of surprise. I felt like someone had sucker-punched me in the gut. What the fuck? "Why didn't you ever tell me?"

She shrugged. "I don't know. It was out of character, something I never thought I'd try—and of course I never imagined you'd start dating him."

I wasn't dating him, but I was too stunned to correct her. Nothing about this situation seemed within the realm of anything I'd ever imagined from my conservative best friend and her ultra-possessive husband. "How was Ben possibly okay with that? I can't imagine him agreeing to share you with another man."

"You have to remember, Ben and I weren't together at that time—not exclusively. And by agreeing to it, he was trying to convince himself that our relationship was just a sensual fling and nothing more. But after that night, everything changed. That night sparked something in him. He realized that he couldn't share me, that he wanted me for himself. And for that reason alone, I'm glad I went through with it. Not to mention, he trusts Braydon completely. I think that was part of the reason why he allowed it."

Wow. There was so much more drama to Ben and Emmy's relationship than I ever imagined. If they could get their happily ever after, there was hope for all of us.

"Say something, Ells." Her eyes were pure agony, lines etched into her forehead like she truly felt horrible she'd slept with Braydon and kept it from me. Good. I wanted to let her suffer for a few seconds more.

"It's so weird to think you know how he is in bed."

She chewed on her lip. "Yes and no. I'm sure you don't want to hear all the gory details, but to be honest, I was more focused on Ben during the whole encounter. The sad, haunted look in his eyes is the thing I remember most."

That filled me with the tiniest amount of relief.

"But yes, trust me," she continued, "I know Braydon is smoking hot and very talented. I knew he'd make some girl very happy someday. I just wasn't her."

I hated that she had firsthand knowledge of just how good he was between the sheets, that she'd seen his sexy piercing. I had to remind myself that they didn't share the off-the-charts chemistry that he and I did. Their relationship was much more like brother and sister, which made it even weirder. I forced it from my mind. Dwelling on it would amount to nothing good. I could either make it into a big, awkward deal or I could accept that it happened and move on. Man, I needed a glass of wine.

After learning so many new things from Emmy—that she had had a threesome with Ben and Braydon and that he was, indeed, fiercely private—I decided to test Braydon a little that night. I wanted to see if he'd invite me to his apartment. I was sharing my body, my time, and my bed with this man. I needed to know that we were on equal footing. Emmy was convinced he was a good guy. We'd see about that. Plus it'd provide a private place for us to talk—if I was brave enough to ask him about his adventures in Paris with Ben and Emmy. I still hadn't decided about that.

I dialed his number and waited while it rang. Braydon answered on the third ring. "Hey, kitten."

"Hi there. Got any plans tonight?" I tried to sound easygoing and light. I didn't want to seem too demanding or pushy. At least not straightaway. But I was hoping to get my way.

"If I did, I'd cancel them for a chance to see your sweet ass."

He could be so sweet and playful when he wanted to. "Actually, I had something in mind. . . ." I let the rest of my thought go unvoiced—a subtle attempt to entice him.

"Hmm. I like that. I'll come over."

"No, I haven't cleaned," I blurted out, losing some of my nerve.

"I don't care about that. I'm not coming over to inspect the vacuum lines in your carpet. I'm coming to see you."

"Yes, but I'm sick of my place. I'd rather go out—or really anywhere but here. How about your place?" I needed to take a stand. We'd only ever met up at my apartment. I crossed my index and middle fingers, awaiting his response. He'd either open up and share a piece of himself with me or he'd blow me off. I had to know.

Braydon was silent for a moment. "I'll get us a hotel room—downtown if you like."

I was completely thrown off by his suggestion. A part of me wanted to argue, but the prospect of not seeing him forced an answer from me before I could think it through. "Sure, why not."

"Great. I'll text you the hotel and room number. Hop in a cab, babe."

"See you soon."

As soon as I hung up the phone I regretted agreeing to his offer. True, I'd said that I wanted to get out of my apartment, but meeting up at a hotel for sex was worse than being in my own space. And I was left wondering, more than ever, why Braydon wouldn't let me into his apartment.

After he texted me the details, I hopped in a cab for the hotel. The bellman pulled open the large glass doors and I entered a decadent lobby with stone floors and crystal chandeliers hanging high above. It made me miss my little apartment and cuddling on my couch with Bray. This made our arrangement feel like something else entirely. I didn't like it. But I entered the elevator and rode up to the seventh floor, conflicted by my intense desire to see him. When I reached the room and knocked, the door was quickly pulled open.

Braydon stood before me in jeans, a white T-shirt, and bare feet. "You made it." He smiled warmly, like this was completely normal. We both had homes in this city. Why were we at a hotel?

"I'm here," I said, my voice devoid of all excitement. Though I was happy to see him and his smile, my head was spinning like a record. Heading inside, I realized he'd rented a suite. It seemed a little over the top for just one night, and I suddenly found myself wondering about his income. Ben certainly made a good living modeling. It appeared Braydon did, too. Not that it mattered to me. I was just curious to learn all I could about this man and his life.

Braydon had set out a bottle of wine and two glasses on the coffee table. "Would you like a glass?" he asked, coming up behind me and wrapping his arms around my waist.

"Sure," I said, trying to sound agreeable. But something about tonight, about being here, felt off. Maybe it was just the sting of rejection that he hadn't invited me over. Either way, I decided I would let it go for now and try to enjoy the evening. Despite the weirdness, it was clear he wanted to be with me. I didn't want to overanalyze that aspect of the situation.

We sat together on the sofa and enjoyed a glass of wine. Braydon filled me in on the photo shoot he'd had earlier with two female models and a live boa constrictor. The women were completely comfortable with the snake and Braydon was the one terrified of the thing, which sent me into a fit of laughter.

"It was longer than the room we were in. Seriously, it's not funny, kitten. It wound itself around my thigh and I about pissed myself."

"Aw, poor baby. Sounds like a tough job." I patted his knee. "Do you need me to make it all better?"

A slow smile curled up his mouth. "That sounds tempting. But not yet. You seem wound up and I need to get you relaxed first." He grinned.

I sipped my wine and looked out at the twinkling city lights below, relishing the moment but also feeling totally confused by it. Our encounters always felt more like romance than a casual arrangement, and it was totally confusing my heart. I didn't want to sit here, drinking wine and watching his gorgeous eyes sparkle while he told me amusing stories, making me fall deeper under his spell. I came into this agreement thinking it'd be more of a *wham, bam, thank you ma'am* situation. And so far it had been anything but. Real feelings were starting to develop and I had no idea if he felt the same way. His hesitation to bring me to his apartment tonight told me probably not. Some girls might think a hotel room was a special date night, but I wasn't that delusional. First, this wasn't a date. It was a private room with a bed where Braydon could fulfill the obligations of the arrangement I was seriously starting to question. Was I insane? Why had I agreed to this?

Then Braydon changed everything. He looked over at me, his gaze darkening with his desire, and I felt like the most beautiful woman in the world. I was addicted to that feeling. This beautiful man wanted me. *Me.* I would give in to my desires tonight. Even if I woke up confused again in the morning.

He moved with the stealth of a panther, slowly setting down his wineglass and turning his body to mine. My heart thumped unevenly and my hands clutched the stem of my glass, desperately needing something to hold on to. Braydon's fingers found mine and he removed the glass from my grasp, setting it with his on the table. "Come here." Taking my hand, he pulled me from the couch. I rose on shaky legs and stood before him. Seeing him dressed so casually, with his bare feet and playful smirk, made me weak in the knees.

I allowed Braydon to lead me into the adjoining bedroom. A large bed dressed in white linens beckoned us, but Braydon released my hand and sat down on the edge and hung his head in his hands.

"Bray?" I carefully stepped closer, wondering what had changed in the course of thirty seconds.

He lifted his head and the crease I saw in his brow was unexpected. I'd never seen him be anything but cool and easygoing. "Do you even want this?" he asked.

"What do you mean?"

"This arrangement—is it what you want? I hate thinking I've lured you into something against your will."

I hadn't done anything I didn't want to do. That much was true. I sat down on the edge of the bed beside him and considered how to answer. The truth was I wanted more, but something told me if I pushed him right now, I'd lose him. He was giving me what he was capable of, and he wanted reassurance that I accepted him and all his limitations. He must have picked up on my contemplative mood out in the living room. "Yes, I want this. I want a real relationship someday, but I know you're not looking for anything steady. I'm not going to let that stop us from hanging out. I like our time together."

His eyes lifted to mine and the little crease in his forehead disappeared. "I do, too."

"Good." It felt strange that I was the one reassuring him about this when I myself felt anything but confident. We had an amazing connection that translated into so much more than just sex. Maybe in time he would see that. I just needed to be patient and go with the flow. Two things I wasn't good at. I scooted a little closer and Braydon brought his hand to my cheek, lovingly stroking my jaw and tucking my hair behind my ear so he could lean down and kiss my neck. His tenderness was unexpected and calmed me instantly. It was crazy how one minute he could rile me up, and then in the next render me speechless.

His soft kisses and the warmth of his mouth instantly brought me back to the moment. His hot tongue licked my neck and his teeth lightly grazed my collarbone. I smiled, knowing that was a favorite spot of his. Soon his mouth drifted toward mine and we were kissing greedily. I loved the taste of him, and I couldn't help myself, I crawled into his lap and straddled him, pushing my hips into his groin and rubbing my tongue against his.

He pulled my shirt over my head and released the clasp of

my bra, his warm hands coming up to hold the weight of my breasts as his thumbs grazed the sensitive peaks. The straining bulge in his jeans told me he was enjoying this every bit as much as I was. Our bodies just fit together. From the way our mouths sought each other's to the way our hips aligned and worked together... it was perfection. He was perfection. And I was in much too deep to stop this now.

After several minutes of his trailing wet kisses all over my breasts, I pushed myself away and crawled from his lap. There was something I wanted to do. I dropped to my knees on the floor in front of him and began working to unbutton his jeans. The dark look in his eyes as he watched me made my breath catch in my throat.

Finally having freed the button, I pulled down his zipper and tugged the jeans from his hips. He wasn't wearing anything underneath. I wasn't sure if it was in anticipation of seeing me tonight, but it was sexy as hell knowing he was bare underneath his denim this entire time. He lifted his hips and the jeans fell down to his knees, freeing him to my kisses. And I didn't waste any time. I'd thought about doing this many times, and even though his piercing intimidated me, I wanted nothing more than to take him in my mouth and make him lose all control.

Wrapping both hands around his generous length, I planted my mouth around him, swirling my tongue against his hot flesh and eliciting a soft groan from him. My tongue flickered against the barbell while I looked up and watched his reaction. His fists were clenched into the bedding and his mouth hung open as he watched me work. I felt seductive and beautiful watching him come apart. He cursed under his breath and pushed my hair out of my face, bringing one hand to the back of my neck and guiding me deeper, showing me how to please him.

"Oh fuck, kitten, that feels incredible."

I felt powerful and doubled my efforts. I licked, kissed, sucked, and stroked him to the best of my ability until his breathing was labored and his chest rumbled with a suppressed groan. Freeing himself from my mouth, Braydon lifted me back onto the bed with him. The hungry look in his eyes told me he was ready for more. He made quick work of stripping me of the last of my clothes and laid me down against the pillows. He'd rushed to strip me naked, but now he was slowing down, taking his time and staring at me with a look of adoration.

"Bray?" I whispered.

"Shh . . ." He pressed a fingertip to my lips. "Just lie back and let me make you come."

I fell back against the pillow once again, breathless and full of conflicting emotions. I wanted this—I wanted him— but I wanted more than just a physical connection. Braydon knew my body better than I did, and he used it to his full advantage. Within moments of his hot mouth closing around my lady parts, I was writhing and coming apart for him.

After he'd finished feasting on me and nibbling on my thighs and hip bones, he grabbed a condom from the bedside table and rolled it on. "I want to fuck you from behind, baby."

"What's your favorite position?" I murmured as I rolled on my stomach, remembering how fond he seemed of this one in particular.

"I think you know." He leaned over me and bit my shoulder.

I yelped and turned my head to glare back at him. He bent his head and tenderly kissed the spot he'd just bitten. "But why do you like it like this?"

"Honestly? I can usually make girls come really easily this way. I think my piercing hits the right spot."

A shiver zipped down my spine. I didn't want to think about him with other women, though his confidence was a turn-on.

"Grab on to that sexy ass while I push slowly inside you."

I did as I was told and Braydon entered me as promised, exquisitely, slowly while pressing sweet, sucking kisses against the back of my neck. He was right about something, this position, this angle . . . it was a deadly combination. My bottom was lifting to meet his thrusts and I was moaning in pleasure into the pillow in front of me.

Once we were both thoroughly satisfied, Braydon disposed of the condom and took me in his arms, kissing my mouth in gentle little nips. I closed my eyes and let the feeling of complete bliss wash over me.

"On a scale of one to sex, how awesome was that?" Braydon chuckled and tucked me securely in against his side. "Shit, kitten. You're amazing."

I lay there, with my heart still pounding and body still clenching with the loss of him, and wondered how I could possibly hold it together. How stupid could I have been to think casual sex with him was going to be enough? I'd always been a commitment, flowers, and romance kind of girl, even if I hadn't been getting the full package from the last few guys I dated. A powerful surge of emotion ripped through me as Braydon held me, murmuring sweet things in my ear.

I felt like crying. I was already falling for him, and there was no way he was going to reciprocate my feelings. He'd made it abundantly clear that whatever was happening between us was just sex.

God, I felt like an idiot.

At times he was so careful and affectionate with me, it felt like anything but a random hookup.

"You want to shower before bed?" he asked.

I hadn't really assumed I'd be spending the night here. I thought this was a place to hook up and then I'd go back home and sleep in my own bed. I didn't have pajamas, my toothbrush . . . not to mention I didn't relish the idea of the walk of shame in the morning, dressed in yesterday's clothes.

I sat up abruptly, knowing this wouldn't work for me. "I wasn't planning on sleeping here."

"Why not?" He patted the space beside him. "King-sized bed. Plenty of space, even for a bed hog like you."

I got out of bed on shaky legs. I knew the scent of this man, his tastes, his preferences, the soft throaty way he cursed when he entered me. Sex brought out far more emotion for me. I couldn't deny it anymore. I wasn't cut out to be one of his arrangements. The act of sex was far more intimate in my view than Braydon believed. It brought a certain closeness that I couldn't shake. I thought of him constantly, remembering the feel of his rough hands on my skin, the way his teeth grazed my neck with every thrust forward. . . .

"Let's face it. We're supposed to be fuck pals, right?" I bit out. His jaw tensed, but he didn't argue. "That's all this is. And we're getting too close, too familiar. I know how you like your eggs, that you like to take a shower after sex and stay in there for exactly seven minutes. I know that you prefer classical music and jazz, which beers are your favorite. . . ."

Braydon sat up on the bed, studying me with curiosity. "This isn't what we agreed to. You're right. I'm sorry."

I wanted to scream at him; I didn't want him to be sorry. I wanted him to take me in his arms, fuck logic, fuck all our rules, and make me his. He said all along he felt this powerful connection between us—wasn't that enough for him to want to be with me?

But instead, he continued watching me with a weary expression while rubbing the back of his neck. "Shall I call you a cab then?"

I shook my head. "No, it's fine. I can grab one right outside the hotel, I'm sure." I just needed out of this room, out of this space that smelled of him, of us, of sex. I needed away from his pretty blue eyes, which always saw too much, before I lost it entirely. Stuffing my feet into my shoes, I dashed for the door. I heard Braydon release a muted curse word just before the door closed. Tears were already swimming in my eyes, so I was thankful for the cover of night.

As soon as I was in the darkened backseat of the yellow cab, I broke down, sobbing uncontrollably while trying to give the poor driver my address. I settled for pointing and stuttering through my tears at the upcoming intersections. The rush of tears had been building for too long, and I could do nothing to stop it. The cab driver handed me a box of tissues and mumbled something in response to my hiccupping my address at him.

I folded my arms around myself, holding tightly. I hated that I could remember how Braydon's hands felt on my skin, the tender way he held me close, the exquisitely slow way he slid deep inside me, the way his breath whispered softly across my lips moments before he kissed me. I scrubbed my hands over my face, wiping away the stupid tears dampening my cheeks. It was foolish to waste tears on him. He and I would never be more. I knew what this was when we started it. He'd pursued me relentlessly, and I'd stupidly agreed to be his fuck friend. I thought I'd be in control, but now I saw that would never be possible. You couldn't not fall for a man like him. He was beautiful, kind, funny, and seriously really fucking good in bed. It really wasn't fair. And now he'd put my life through a blender. He was all I thought about, everything I wanted. And I couldn't have him.

I pulled in a shaky breath and forced myself to hold it together. Soon the cab was pulling to a stop in front of my building. I shoved thirty dollars at the driver and climbed from the car, my sore body cruelly reminding me of my intimate encounter with Braydon.

Once inside my silent and familiar apartment, I padded to my bedroom, undressed, and climbed under the covers. It was obvious I wasn't cut out for casual sex. Yet I knew with absolute certainty I wasn't doing anything to stop Braydon's pursuit of me.

8

The following day, I woke up with a clearer sense of myself. I was glad I hadn't stayed in that hotel room when I'd felt uncomfortable. Waking up in my own bed had done me some good. I felt the tiniest bit more in control. I was in too deep with this arrangement with Braydon and I needed to maintain some semblance of control. Later that day, Emmy called.

"Hey, are you almost ready?" Emmy's voice crackled through a bad connection on her cell.

"Ready for what?" I asked.

It was clear she didn't hear me because she kept right on with her questions. "And are you guys driving separately or is the limo picking you up?"

"Emmy, what are you talking about?"

The static in the phone crackled and faded, and Emmy went silent. "Oh. Shit, Ells, I'm sorry, I just assumed you were coming tonight with Braydon."

"Coming where?" Now my curiosity was piqued. Apparently they were all headed somewhere tonight. And I wasn't invited.

"It's um, a gala honoring the best male models in the business. Both Ben and Braydon received nominations for awards."

"Oh." It sounded pretty significant. A huge honor for Braydon, and he hadn't mentioned a thing. I guess that told me where I ranked on his list of priorities. Getting his tux cleaned was above *Call Ellie* on his to-do list. "It's fine, Emmy. Have fun tonight."

"Nonsense, put your best cocktail dress on and throw your hair up into one of those pretty up-dos you're so good at. You'll come with me and Ben. I'm sure it won't be a problem."

I was so not okay with accepting a pity invite. And I certainly didn't want to play third wheel all night. Hell no. If Braydon had wanted to see me tonight, he would have invited me. I had standards. Shit, I wasn't going to show up and beg for his attention. Though the idea of wearing a sexy cleavage-baring dress to tease him was intriguing, I would never go where I wasn't welcome. "Emmy, I'm fine. Don't worry about it. Go to the gala, have fun, and don't give it another thought. I just ordered a pizza, and I'm in yoga pants cruising Netflix. I'm cool with a night in by myself." Especially since I was planning to have a good cry once I hung up the phone.

"This is awkward, I'm so sorry. I shouldn't have said anything. I just assumed you'd be joining Braydon as his plus one."

"No, he never mentioned it. It's totally cool, sweetie." Lies. All lies. I was crushed. It hurt like hell, but no one needed to know my inner turmoil. "I told you we're not dating." And he seemed reluctant to be seen with me in public. His comment about walking red carpets alone came rushing back to taunt me. "Listen, have a great time, take lots of pictures, and I hope Ben wins." I forced a smile onto my face to try to sound cheery.

"Thanks, I hope either Ben or Braydon wins. That'd be fantastic!"

I chuckled, realizing a win for Ben would really stick it to their nemesis, Fiona. It would show that he no longer needed the backing of a big modeling agency. "Have fun tonight."

"You too," Emmy said, a hint of sadness in her voice.

I hated myself for it, but after talking to her I sulked for the remainder of the night. After overdoing it on ice cream, I felt sick and anxious. I finally decided to just call it a night and go to bed, knowing I'd never be able to live with myself if I purposely waited up for his call.

When I was finally drifting off to sleep, my phone chimed with a new text. I reached frantically for my phone, hoping it was him. My heart kicked up in my chest, beating in a steady rhythm.

Braydon: You asleep?

So it was a less-than-inspiring text, but still, it proved he was thinking of me. A quick check of the clock informed me it was already two in the morning. I considered not responding— letting him wonder if maybe I was out on the town. I clutched my phone in the darkness, debating what to do. I realized by not responding I'd only be punishing myself. I wanted to talk to him. Besides, Emmy probably mentioned my night in with Netflix.

Me: Not yet. What's up?

There. I kept it casual and breezy. Not overly needy.

Braydon: I was thinking about you.

A sleepy smile curled my lips upward. Okay, so he was being sweet. Rather than chastise him for not inviting me along, or this apparent late-night booty call, I decided to play nice.

Me: How was tonight?

Braydon: Fine. I didn't win. Neither did Ben. I went to the afterparty and got trashed, though. And I'm pretty sure Ben and Emmy fucked in the coat closet.

I rolled my eyes. That sounded like them. I wanted to ask why he didn't tell me about the event, but didn't want him to know I was hurt by the lack of invite. Things between us were supposed to be easy and light.

Braydon: I want you.

I stared at his words, deciding what I wanted. Earlier, I probably would've jumped at the attention. Now I was feeling stronger and more in control.

Me: I'm in bed.

Braydon: I'll join you.

Me: Not tonight.

I waited for him to write something back, to try and coax me into it in a cute, sexy way, but no reply ever came.

I was thankful our conversation had been through text, rather than face-to-face. I knew my hurt and contempt would've risen to the surface. He would have read me like a book. He had a knack for that. I just didn't understand why he didn't invite me along tonight as a friend. I knew we weren't an item. He'd made that abundantly clear. Something nagged in the back of my head and I vowed to get to the bottom of Braydon's strange, secretive behavior—first about his apartment and also about being seen in public with a woman.

I rolled over, hugging a pillow to my chest, and went to sleep. I'd figure out my next move in the morning.

I took myself out to Sunday brunch the next day, putting on an air of confidence and reminding myself I didn't need a man. I dined at a pricey neighborhood restaurant in a dress and a strand of pearls. While I happily sipped a mimosa and nibbled on chocolate chip pancakes, I celebrated myself. I was a strong, confident woman. A scientist, for heaven's sake. I didn't need a man like Braydon Kincaid to make me feel worthy.

Stuffing a bite of sausage into my mouth, I vowed then and there I would make him communicate better with me. I deserved that much, at least. I needed to know where I stood with him, what this was between us, and why I couldn't go to his apartment. I swallowed the bite and washed it down with the rest of the delicious orange juice–and-champagne combination, feeling so much better and in control for the first time in days.

On my walk back home, Emmy called and I picked up my phone.

"Hey, you busy today?" she asked.

"Nope."

"Wanna come to a shoot with me? Ben and Bray are being photographed together for a small local magazine. I thought it might be fun to see."

I wondered if this was her attempt at fixing things between me and Braydon after the gala snub.

"Sure." I'd love the chance to see Braydon at work.

"Cool. I'll pick you up in fifteen."

"Make it twenty. I'm not quite home yet. Wait. What should I wear?" I wanted to look stylish. It wasn't every day you crashed a photo shoot.

"Doesn't matter. We'll be behind the scenes, remember?"

"Of course." I was being silly. But that didn't stop me from putting on my most fashionable black ankle pants, cute black and sparkly ballet flats, and a designer cream-colored silk blouse. I fixed my long dark locks in a low ponytail and added lip gloss, then studied myself in the mirror. There. At least I felt more put-together. I was ready.

When Emmy arrived, she sent a text letting me know and I jogged down the four flights of stairs to the waiting black sedan chauffeured by Henry.

"You look cute," Emmy noted, looking me over.

I felt cute, too. But mostly just excited to surprise Braydon. There was no reason things needed to feel weird between us. We just needed to talk things over. I was convinced we could fix this.

"Ready?"

"Yup."

I listened while Emmy filled me in on the details of their charity. Things were going quite well and Ben was taking on fewer modeling jobs to devote more time to their very worthy cause of helping children in need. It was quite admirable.

Soon we were rolling to a stop by an old, run-down building. It didn't look like much, but I quickly saw its potential. The photographer was using the rough brick façade as a rugged backdrop to capture his subjects. Ben and Braydon were stationed against the wall, each striking brilliant poses as the photographer clicked away. They were dressed casually—each in jeans, Braydon in a simple black T-shirt, and Ben in a white button-down.

Emmy and I approached from the far side, staying out of their line of vision, not wanting to distract them. This world was entirely new to me, but Emmy seemed a bit more comfortable, waving to the makeup artist and moving with authority to the sidelines.

We chatted with a set designer, the editor for the magazine, and nibbled on snacks from the catering table. While Emmy went to talk with the makeup artist she seemed to know from another shoot, I sat down on a brick ledge near the edge of the building to watch the shoot. I didn't realize a photo shoot could last so long, and just when I'd grown bored with waiting around for Braydon to finish, a bubbly blonde with bouncy curls plopped down beside me.

"He's stunning, isn't he?" I assumed she meant Ben because he was the more well known of the two, but a quick glance up told me her gaze was pinned on Braydon.

"Yes, he is." No denying that fact. The man was frickin' sex on a stick. Lickable in every way. And I would know. Just the memory of our naughty hotel room encounter made my skin heat up.

Her smile faltered ever so slightly as she sized me up. Pushing her thick blond curls over one shoulder, she offered me her hand. "I'm Katrina."

"Hi, I'm Ellie." I returned her handshake. "Are you one of the . . . set workers?" I didn't know the right terms. My newbie status was obvious.

She laughed a light musical sound. "No. Just . . . an admirer."

Oh. "Of Ben Shaw or Braydon Kincaid?" I wondered out loud.

"Braydon." The familiar way his name rolled from her lips set off a warning bell in my head. "What about you?" she asked.

I flushed pink. How did I explain our arrangement to a perfect stranger? "Oh, I've been, um, sort of seeing him," I said softly.

"Really?" This seemed to surprise her, her eyebrows lifting high up her forehead.

I couldn't get over the unmistakable feeling that something wasn't quite right. "Do you know him?" She'd said she was just an admirer, but I sensed they had a past.

"Yes. He and I . . ." she stopped herself. "Doesn't matter. But I know how he can be, and commitment is tough for him."

I nodded, spellbound. I wondered if she'd been one of his past arrangements. My heart pumped wildly in my chest.

She pulled a scrap of paper from her purse and scribbled something down on it before thrusting it at me. "My phone number and email. If you ever want to talk."

"Thanks." I tucked the note inside my wallet.

Emmy approached and offered me her hand. "Ready? The boys are done."

I accepted her hand and allowed her to pull me to standing. I hadn't realized they were already through. Something about meeting Katrina, and the way her eyes had followed Braydon's every movement, made my scalp tingle. A quick glance back told me my new friend was already gone—without a trace, by the looks of it. Strange. Shaking away the eerie feeling, I followed Emmy. The guys emerged a few minutes later and Braydon's brows crinkled when he spotted me. He looked agitated.

"Everything okay?" he asked as he approached.

"Yes, we came to see you guys. Nice work."

The tension in his face fell away just slightly. "Oh. Cool. Sorry." He scrubbed a hand through his messy hair. "There was just a little issue. Security had to remove someone from the set." Emmy's concerned eyes met Ben's. "Everything's fine now," Braydon explained.

Weird.

I suddenly felt strange being here. Not only was this the first time I'd been around the three of them since learning about their steamy night in Paris, but Braydon hadn't invited me here today—Emmy had. And I got the distinct feeling I wasn't exactly welcome. My plan to push him to talk died when I saw his serious expression. Now was not the time. I shifted my weight, hitching my purse up higher on my shoulder. "Well, I've got a lot to do today. I should probably hit it."

Emmy shot me a confused glare. "I thought you were free all day?"

"I've got errands to run, I need to go to the store, do laundry, get groceries, return an overdue book to the library. . . ." I stopped myself from spewing any further lies.

Braydon's posture relaxed a bit and he leaned down to give me a hug. "I'll see you later, yeah?"

"Sure," I murmured, my agitation growing. Braydon wasn't happy to see me. He didn't appreciate my effort. He was so confusing, it made my stomach hurt. Coming here had been a bad idea. I turned and fled, heading for the nearest cab or subway station I could find. I just wanted out of there.

That evening when Braydon texted me, asking to come over, I immediately said yes. I'd let him know what was on my mind when he arrived. I had to, for my sanity's sake. I couldn't keep walking around day after day, not knowing. When he arrived at my apartment, bottle of wine in hand, I ushered him inside, my resolve weakening at the sight of this handsome man. He was dressed casually in a pair of dark jeans, a vintage tee, and his beat-up Converse, as he usually was. He looked frickin' adorable.

He kissed me briefly then set about opening the wine and pouring us each a glass. I bit my cheek to avoid asking him about the gala or his strange behavior on the set of the photo shoot. *Let it go, Ellie. Move on*, I begged myself silently. There are more important things to discuss.

"Here you go, gorgeous." He handed me a glass of ruby-colored wine. "Shall we sit?" He motioned to the living room and I led the way, nestling into my couch, which was worn in all the right places. Braydon sat down next to me but left enough room between us so that we could carry on a conversation naturally.

"Listen, I think we need to talk," I began.

"Yes, we do," he agreed, watching me thoughtfully over the rim of his wineglass.

"Okay, you go first."

"Nope. Not yet. Tell me what's on your mind."

I chewed on my lower lip. Did I have the courage to do this? Making the split-second decision that I wasn't yet ready to probe into anything deeper—like where he and I stood—I blurted the first thing that came to mind. "I know about the threesome."

Braydon didn't even blink. "Am I in trouble?"

I considered it. But it happened before he met me. It'd be completely unfair to be mad at him about something that had happened in his past. "No, you're not. I was just surprised is all. I wish you had told me."

"Emmy told you, I take it?"

"She knew about your piercing, and when I pressed about how she knew . . . she told me the story." He nodded, like he understood this wasn't something that could be kept secret forever. It had to come out eventually. Emmy and I were best friends. "Is it weird for you now? Being around Ben and Emmy?" I asked.

He shook his head. "Nah. I don't really think about it. I knew it was a one-time thing. Ben and I had done that type of thing before, and it was never a big deal. It was something we did for fun."

He and I had very different ideas of fun. "Is that something you'd want to . . . would you share me with someone?"

"No." His voice was firm. "I have no desire to do that again. And I have no interest in sharing your sweet little body with anyone."

Satisfied with his answer, I knew I had to let it go. Though I knew the next time we were all together, I would have a hard time not picturing the three of them in compromising positions, wondering about the mechanics of how it all went down. I shook my head, clearing my mind. Braydon had said there was something he wanted to talk to me about, and I still had to work up what I wanted to say about some of our bigger issues. *Focus, Ellie.* "Okay, now that the weirdness is out of the way . . . what did you want to talk about?"

He pushed a lock of hair behind my ear and grinned down at me, as if he was proud about how mature I was being about his past. "I'm leaving for Maui next week and I'll be gone for two weeks."

"Oh." Two whole weeks without any texts and visits from Braydon to look forward to? It hurt more than it should. The wine churned in my stomach.

"I've given it a lot of thought, and I'd like you to come with me."

"What?" That wasn't at all what I was expecting. I thought he was going to chastise me for getting too close, for wanting things he'd told me we'd never have. "Ben and Emmy will be there, too. I thought it might be fun."

"I can't. I have to work, Braydon."

"I know, but I thought perhaps you could use a vacation. And I thought it'd be nice to have you there." He smiled at me warmly, making my heart flutter erratically.

All the things I wanted to say to him about his reluctance to be seen with me went out the window. He was inviting me to Hawaii. That spoke louder than anything, didn't it?

"I do have a week of vacation time saved up." The idea of spending a week in the sun with Braydon, Ben, and Emmy sounded heavenly. "I'll ask my boss about it tomorrow."

"That's a good girl." I smiled at the endearment, gazing up at him like a lovesick fool. "I work better when I'm having regular orgasms, so you being there will be very helpful." He chuckled.

My stomach dropped, and I let out an exasperated sigh. That was why he invited me? I couldn't be some kept woman, a mistress hidden away in his hotel room. I had a job, a life, a brain. I was more than just a vagina for him to sink into whenever he pleased. "That's why you want me there? Newsflash: I'm not just a warm hole to be used for your enjoyment." I felt like punching him, but I kept my composure.

"Of course you're not," he quickly recovered. "I'm sorry I made you feel that way. The truth is, I love hanging out with you. You're fun as shit, and we have great sex. I know you're not going to deny that."

"Well, no," I murmured weakly.

"I'd like you to come on the trip with me because I think it would be good for both of us."

"We'll see." I wanted to be sure that I was protecting myself and could handle an entire week with him.

"Well, think about it." He rose to his feet and, to my complete surprise, left the apartment without saying good-bye. *What the hell?* His wineglass sat untouched on the coffee table where he'd left it. Was he trying to give me space to think, or was this some kind of test?

The entire week passed without a single word from Braydon. I hadn't texted or called him either, but he was the guy, he was supposed to chase me, right? I knew he was leaving for Hawaii in two days—I found out from Emmy. And I hated myself for it, but I went ahead and inquired about the time off with my boss. She'd said it was totally fine and probably long overdue. Which only frustrated me more. I could have the time off if I wanted it. I just didn't want to give in so easily. Braydon hadn't clarified if he'd be paying my way, if we'd share a hotel room, or what sort of rules would apply to this part of our *arrangement*. I had enough money in my savings to cover the flight and hotel, but still—I hated all these questions swirling in my brain. I wished there were a guidebook for this. If you're invited on vacation to be someone's fuck buddy, what are the expectations?

My cell phone rang and I sprinted across my apartment, lunging for it. "Hello?"

"Hey, Ells," Emmy said.

"Oh. Hi."

She laughed. "Geez, nice to hear from you, too."

"Sorry, I just, thought it might be . . . never mind."

"Bray?"

"Yeah."

She sighed. "You guys still aren't talking?"

"Nope."

She grumbled something unintelligible into the phone. "Sheesh, you two are more stubborn than Ben and I ever were."

"What's that supposed to mean?" I picked at a hangnail on my thumb.

"It means you both want each other, yet you're too damn stubborn to admit it and take what you want."

"So what should I do?"

"Suck it up and call him. Tell him you want to go to Hawaii."

"I can't do that, Emmy."

"Why the hell not? Are you insane? Piña coladas on the

beach . . . warm sand . . . sun . . . me . . . hello? It's gonna be awesome."

I laughed at her enthusiasm. "It does sound nice. Let me think about it."

"Don't think for too long. We leave the day after tomorrow."

"Trust me, I'm well aware." I paced my apartment, trying to figure out what to do. Things between me and Braydon were totally in the gray, but I wanted to go to Hawaii with my best friend and our two men. And I had the time off work. Why the fuck not?

"I need a bikini wax and a pedicure," I mumbled into the phone.

Emmy squealed. "Oh hush. That's what razors are for, and we'll get a pedicure together at the hotel. I'm sure there's a spa nearby."

Gosh, her life was easy. "Okay," I said with a nod. "I better pack then."

"Hop to it, girlie!"

"Will do. And hey, don't mention anything to Ben or Braydon yet, okay?"

"Sure thing, babe," Emmy said, though sounding skeptical.

As I hung up the phone, a little plan hatched in my head. Surprising Braydon on the airplane . . . initiating our membership into the mile-high club just after ascent. I giggled devilishly and skipped to my bedroom to pack. Maybe I just needed to give him a bit more time to develop the feelings I already had. This was new territory for him, and it was a big step that he'd invited me to travel with him, and I needed to accept the invitation in the spirit it was given. My confidence increased as I gave myself a little pep talk. Things would work themselves out.

Heaping mountains of clothes on my bed, I had all the major travel groups accounted for: bathing suits, sundresses, shorts, tanks, sandals, a pair of heels, a cocktail dress in case we did anything upscale, and a sweatshirt since it got so cold on planes. After it was all shoved into my largest suitcase, I settled on the couch with my laptop to purchase my airfare. I texted Emmy to find out which flight they were on, and while I waited for her to respond, I emailed my boss, letting her know that I was taking her up on that offer for a week off after all. My stomach was a mess of nervous energy, and I felt like bouncing off the walls of my tiny apartment. I hadn't felt so happy and alive in a long time. Braydon and the newness of our affair had that effect on me. It certainly was good for the libido. I just hadn't decided if he was good for the rest of me—namely, my heart.

My phone chimed a second later and Emmy's response burst my bubble. Crap. She, Ben, and Braydon were all seated in first class.

Me: Shit, I can't afford first class. Looks like I'll be sitting all by my lonesome. ☹

Emmy: Oh hush! Tell Braydon and he'll pay for your ticket. Stop being stubborn, remember??

I considered her words. But I wasn't being stubborn. Not

this time. This time, I wanted to stand on my own two feet and show him I was committed to being there and taking him up on his offer, despite everything we'd been through over the past week. It wasn't every day a man invited me to join him on vacation. And I'd all but snubbed him. He'd left quietly without a word. And now it'd been utter silence. I remembered something my mom told me once: Men are more sensitive than you'd think. I wondered if I'd hurt his feelings by refusing his offer. It was a big step for him to invite me to Hawaii. I would make this right. I had to—I needed to see where things were going between us.

9

I spotted Ben and Emmy straightaway in first class only a couple rows back from the front. Across the aisle from them was Braydon—with a pretty redhead fawning all over him. My heart pinched painfully in my chest.

He'd invited someone else?

I needed off this plane. But I was stuck, with someone in front of me wrestling her luggage into the overhead compartment and a whole line of people behind me waiting to board. I drew a shaky breath and continued forward. It was all I could do.

He'd said no one else could be inside me, and that he'd refrain, too. Apparently that had gone out the window when a piece of ass came sniffing around. Hot anger burned through me. I wanted to shove the perky little redhead away from him and slug him in the face for good measure. I'd never felt quite so possessive over a man. I wanted to yank that bitch away from him by her hair. Instead, I took a calming breath and cleared my throat.

Braydon's eyes snapped up to mine. "Kitten?"

I smirked. *Busted, buddy.*

His mouth curled up in a smile. Not the least bit distraught about being discovered with his new little toy. What an ass.

"I was going to surprise you." I looked down at the dirty, multicolored carpeting, unable to meet his brilliant blue eyes.

"You sure did." He stood and came closer to where I was wedged between the aisle and his row of seats.

"I can see that. I didn't know you'd have someone else with you." My eyes landed on the redhead who stood just two feet away, watching us with a pout.

"Oh, Megan? No, she's the photographer's assistant. She just spotted me. We didn't know we were on the same flight."

Oh. "Hi," I offered, feeling stupid.

"Hi!" She beamed, grinning at me. "I better get back to my seat." She turned and headed for the rear of the plane, waiting in the queue of people as they inched their way back.

I said hi to Ben and Emmy, still feeling strange for showing up on the flight out of the blue like this. But I was so thoroughly rattled at thinking Braydon had invited someone else, I felt like I was floating above my body, witnessing everything through a thick haze.

"Come here, girly." Braydon opened his arms and pulled me into a massive hug.

I staggered against his chest, inhaling his unique scent—

soap and masculine goodness. Relief washed over me that he hadn't invited someone to replace me. God, my nerves were shot already. I took a step back, needing some space. "You sure you want me here?"

"She's a groupie, nothing more. I invited you, didn't I?"

"Yes," I murmured.

"Then get your hot ass over here." He tugged me down to his lap and caged me in with his arms around my waist. "There, that's better." He pressed his mouth to my neck and gave me a gentle bite.

I yelped softly.

Emmy shot me a glare. "You two better behave on this flight."

Braydon's smile turned serious. "She's right, we better buckle up." He fixed the seat belt around us both.

"Braydon," I laughed, trying to maneuver myself out of his lap. "We can't share a seat." As much as I wanted to.

"Fine." He pouted. He pressed the call button in the panel above us and a flight attendant appeared a moment later. Braydon explained that I'd surprised him on the flight but had secured a seat in coach. He turned his pretty blue eyes at her and asked if it was possible to bump me up to first class. She scurried off to check the status of the flight to see if it was full. There was no one in the seat next to him for the time being, but that could change since people were still filtering onto the plane. She returned a moment later with a new ticket for me, indicating my new seat, next to Braydon. Wow, being ridiculously good-looking had its perks. I moved from his lap and settled in. I'd never flown first class before and I was more than a little excited. This was old hat for him, Ben, and Emmy, but I found it all incredibly exciting. I was practically bouncing in the seat with excitement. I was really doing it. And I felt nearly delirious about spending a week in Hawaii with Braydon.

I buckled myself into the plush leather seat for the eleven-hour flight while the attendant delivered us the drink of our choice and a mixed tin of salted almonds. I could get used to this lifestyle.

"I would have bought you a ticket if I'd known you were coming," Braydon said, nuzzling into my neck again.

"Then I couldn't have surprised you."

"Thank you for that." He smiled at me sincerely and my world was complete. God, that dimple of his would be the death of me.

Once we landed in Hawaii, our foursome was bubbling with energy, despite the overly long flight. We were giddy and ready to enjoy a fruity cocktail and feel the ocean breeze caress our skin. Ben had arranged ahead of time for a car and driver, so we followed the uniformed driver holding a sign that read "Mr. Shaw." Braydon couldn't keep his hands off me in the car. Ben sat in the front seat with the driver, which left me wedged in the middle seat between Braydon and Emmy. Braydon's lips hovered behind my ear.

"I'm so glad you decided to come."

"Me too," I admitted softly. "I hope you're okay with

sharing a room because I didn't make any hotel accommo-
dations."

"Hmmm." He tapped his index finger against his lips as
if deep in thought. "You in my bed? Fuck it, I'll deal." He
grinned down at me. "Silly girl." Then he dropped a kiss on
my mouth.

Our hotel was right on the water and the sun was sinking into the ocean when we arrived. It was absolutely stunning, especially the expansive marble-floored lobby, with its
dark rattan furniture and sculptures of mermaids and other
sea creatures. It was island-chic, and I very much approved.
I hadn't really been on an adult vacation like this. Growing
up, my family vacations consisted of camping in upstate New
York or driving to the coast for a day trip. This was a whole
other world, and I immediately relaxed into the easy island
vibe. I could definitely handle this.

Once checked in, we dropped our bags and agreed to
meet in the hotel bar in ten minutes. Braydon and I sat waiting for Ben and Emmy for a good forty minutes, sipping fruit
cocktails and laughing as we watched a group of tourists.
When they finally made it downstairs, we were on our third
drink and Emmy's just-fucked hair was a dead giveaway about
what they'd been up to. As if I had any doubts.

"Cheers to island sex," Braydon announced as they
walked up, their cheeks still flushed. "Was it good?"

We all burst into laughter. "Be nice to my wife." Ben
curled a protective hand around Emmy's hip.

"Hey, I'm just proud that you guys didn't christen the plane and join the mile-high club," I said as they took their seats. "You kept us waiting, and now I'm starving." I picked up a menu.

"Yeah, we worked up quite an appetite as well," Ben said as he smiled at his blushing bride. Lord, they were ridiculous. We hadn't intended to have dinner at this little island-themed bar, but since we were here and hungry, we all gave in and found appetizers on the menu to share: deep-fried calamari, shrimp cocktail, and other yummy island favorites. Soon, we'd downed several rounds of drinks and were all tipsy and full.

"Let's go for a walk on the beach. I need to dip my toes in the sand," Emmy suggested.

"Sounds great," I chimed in.

After an overdue visit to the restroom, we met the boys at the front of the restaurant. They'd settled the bill with our server and were standing near the hostess booth waiting for us. The poor hostess across from them looked like her eyes were going to pop out of their sockets. Her mouth was hanging open and her fingers were gripping the wooden podium in front of her, like she was fighting to remain standing. I knew the feeling. I elbowed Emmy in the ribs and gestured to the girl who was beyond smitten with our two men. They were a feast for the eyes. They'd yet to notice the girl, and were laughing and talking among themselves. They looked beautiful. Sheesh, they were beautiful. Two of the most sought-after men in the world. And they were with us. Pride surged through me.

Emmy and I shared a knowing, devilish glance, each with the same naughty thought. We strutted up to our men and planted a big kiss on their respective mouths. Braydon's arms encircled my waist and my eyes slid closed. I forgot about the hostess—hell, I forgot my own name as I lost myself in the kiss. Emmy clearing her throat next to us was the only thing that pulled me away. Screw seeing the beach—the ocean had been there for centuries and it'd likely still be there tomorrow. I wanted to be alone with Braydon.

"Bray . . ." I tugged his hand. His eyes met mine and he must have read me like a book. He did have a striking talent for that.

"We'll catch up with you guys tomorrow," he said to Ben and Emmy.

"Are you sure?" Emmy asked.

"The beach will be there," Braydon said, reflecting my own thoughts. "My kitten and I need to celebrate."

Emmy's eyes danced on mine. I could tell she was truly happy for me. I felt warm and tipsy and decidedly happy that I'd come to Hawaii. If only I could have predicted how wrong I'd be about this trip.

10

After a room service breakfast of fragrant local Kona coffee and delicious pineapple tarts, I changed into a pair of shorts and a tank top. Emmy and I had plans while the guys worked. I leaned over and planted a kiss on Braydon's mouth as he sat in a lounge chair on our lanai. "I'm meeting Emmy for pedicures. I'll see you after lunch?"

His hand found my hip and he pulled me closer for another kiss, like he wasn't ready to say good-bye just yet. Even though we'd made love last night and this morning. Things were starting to feel more solid between us, and to say I liked it would've been a giant understatement. "Mmm," he confirmed, his mouth refusing to leave mine.

"Good luck today."

He patted my butt and released his hold. "Have fun with Emmy and make sure you charge your pedicure to my room. I want to treat you."

"You don't have to do that."

"I know. I want to. Now go, have fun." He patted my butt and sent me on my way.

After a morning of having my feet scrubbed and my toes polished, Emmy and I ate lunch by the pool and flipped through gossip magazines. We sunned ourselves while sipping frozen fruity concoctions. It was absolute perfection. I loved that we were comfortable enough that we didn't need to fill the silence with mindless chatter. We just laid back, basked in the relaxing sounds of the waves crashing, and took in the sun's warming rays. I couldn't quite believe this was my life. I was here, on the island of Maui, with my bestie and our men, who were two of the world's top male models. It was kind of crazy.

By three o'clock we were all sunned out and in need of some shade and a shower to rinse off the sweat and suntan lotion. Plus, we figured the guys would be back from their shoot by now, and though neither of us admitted it, I think we both missed them. Lord help me, it'd only been a handful of hours since I'd last seen Braydon, and I already craved more. I was thankful he'd invited me, and that I'd let my stubbornness go and followed him here.

Braydon returned to the room when I was in the shower. At first I feared it was housekeeping, but I heard his deep, sexy voice calling out for his *kitten* and I beamed. He was back. "In here, lover," I called.

The bathroom door opened and a cloud of steam escaped, revealing my beautiful man standing before me in just a pair of baby blue board shorts slung low on his hips. Heaven help me. My eyes slid from his rock-hard chest to his defined abs to the fine trail of hair disappearing under the waistband of his shorts. He looked edible. And judging by the adorable smirk tugging up his full mouth, he knew it. "Care for some company?" he asked.

Without waiting for my response, Braydon's hands found the tie holding up his trunks and gave it a tug, releasing the knot. I swallowed heavily, captivated by his beauty and breathless to see all of him revealed. Treating me to a warm chuckle that I felt vibrate against my skin, Braydon let the swim trunks fall down his legs and stepped out of them. He was already semi-erect, and I fought the urge to reach out and touch him as he entered the glass-enclosed shower built for two.

"How was your day?" he asked, taking me into his arms. I rested my head against his chest and exhaled slowly.

"Perfect. Especially now that you're back. How did your shoot go?"

"Fine. Nothing too exciting. We were in a eucalyptus forest, though. It smelled fantastic. You would have liked it." Braydon grabbed the body wash and began lathering up my back as I leaned against his solid chest. And soon our innocent shower time turned into something much more fun.

We made love in the shower until the water started to run cold and then escaped, giggling, teeth chattering, into the warmth of our big, fluffy bed.

We remained there for the rest of the afternoon, talking, touching, and kissing, and while most of me felt happy and complete, part of me feared this would all come to an end. Did Braydon feel these things, too?

As the afternoon sun fell away, we still had no desire to move from our warm nest. In the dim light, Braydon watched me for some time. I fought to keep my expression neutral, to ease the worry lines from my forehead, but I could tell he knew something was different. Something had changed between us. I blinked and looked down, toying with the edge of the blanket I'd pulled up to shield my naked body.

"How are you feeling?" he asked, his voice a low, throaty rasp in the darkness.

I swallowed the nervous tension in my throat. "Fine," I lied. "Just tired."

A slow smile overtook his face. "I wore you out, huh?"

I nodded. "Something like that." He didn't need to know the truth. Hell, I didn't even want to face it. I was falling hard for this man. This man who'd made it abundantly clear that he and I were only about the physical. And I'd agreed. I had no one but myself to blame for this beautiful mess I was in.

"Come here." He opened his arms for me to come closer and I obeyed, nestling against his warm body.

We were all wrong for each other, but I fought to quiet my brain and just let him hold me. When he was gentle like this, it was all I could do to fold my body into his and just let him soothe me. He had a way with me that no one else did. His clean, masculine scent, the way my head nestled so perfectly under his chin with our exaggerated differences in height ... it was all too perfect. And that scared the ever-loving shit out of me.

Strong muscles enveloped me as Braydon's arms closed

around me. We fit together too perfectly. It was impossible not to notice. My sick little brain grasped on to that fact and refused to let go.

"You feel so perfect in my arms, kitten." I relaxed into him at his sweet admission. At least I wasn't the only one who noticed. His large palm slid down my hip and cupped my bottom, his gentle caresses becoming less and less innocent. I felt his thick length nudge at my thigh as he hardened. "It's crazy how badly I want you," he whispered.

I loved knowing I affected him, even if it was just physical. I let myself sink into him, taking all I could get of my sweet nothing.

The next three days passed in much the same way. Braydon and I hung out in our room, and when he went to work Emmy and I hit the beach. My skin was developing a nice golden hue, and each day I looked forward to Braydon's return. We hadn't had time for sightseeing or excursions, and to my disappointment, we hadn't even gone out for a proper dinner together. I hadn't been able to wear any of the cute sundresses I'd brought or explore any of the resort's many restaurants. He ordered in every meal, insisting on room service and that we eat either out on our lanai or in the living room of the suite. I couldn't help but feel disappointed.

As I sat waiting for Braydon to return from his business dinner with the photographer and designer, I became more and more wound up. Emmy had confirmed that she and Ben were at the same dinner, even though Braydon had made it sound like it'd be some dull thing he had to do for work. Why didn't he just bring me along as a friend? Why was every little thing so difficult with him? I shared my time, my body, my apartment, everything I had, and he couldn't share the simplest of things with me. I gave him a mile and he struggled to give me an inch. It was beyond infuriating. I was starting to feel like he was hiding me out in this hotel room, placating me with food and sex. It wasn't nearly enough. My temper raged the more and more I sat pondering it.

By the time he arrived back at the room, I was livid, and I was ready to let him have it. I didn't move from the couch, didn't even look up when he entered the hotel room. The TV was off, as were the lights. I was just sitting there in the dark, stewing over this one-sided relationship I'd built up in my head.

"Ellie?" he asked, his tone unsure and worried. He crossed the room and turned on a lamp. Good. He knew something was wrong. Maybe he even regretted his actions. Yeah right, but a girl could hope.

"Is everything okay?" He sat down beside me.

No. In fact nothing was okay. I was good enough to fuck, but not good enough to even take outside. "Did you have a nice dinner?"

His blue eyes squinted at mine. "Yeah. It was fine. Is that what this is about? Me going to dinner?"

He made it sound so trivial, but it was so much more than that to me. I wouldn't deny how I felt. "I feel hidden away in this room—stashed and out of sight like your luggage or dirty laundry. I just expected we'd spend more time together—on the beach, going out . . . I don't, doing couple stuff. Stupid of me, huh?" This was it. The final straw. It was one thing to have a mutually beneficial sexual relationship, but it was quite another to feel used and cast aside by a man I was giving myself to completely. I didn't care what he'd said—it was more than just physical between us, and if he couldn't see that, he wasn't worth his weight in salt.

With my heart sinking lower in my chest, I released a heavy sigh. How did I let this happen? How could I have been so foolish? I wanted to be the one who cooked for him, who rubbed his back, played with his hair, and listened to all the nonsense about his day. I wanted to be his somebody, his plus one. But he was keeping me at a distance.

His inability to commit, his indecisive nature, the fact that he wouldn't even take me for a simple dinner, all meant I shouldn't be falling for him. He was all wrong for me. I hated how broken he was. I couldn't take any more of this. I was left to feel lonely and exhausted. Each time we'd shared a playful laugh, each time his mouth quirked up when I put him in his place, I'd fallen for him a little harder. And let's not even get started on the responses he evoked from my body. Things in that category were downright explosive.

He pressed his fingertips against his temples and let out a heavy sigh. "You know I don't mean to make you feel like that. It's just . . ." he hesitated.

"Yeah, I know. You won't go out in public with me—in New York *and* here—and you won't date me or commit to

a relationship. Yet you expect me to be faithful and monoga-
mous, right?"

He looked down at the floor, unable to argue.

A hollow feeling filled my chest. I hated how much faith
I'd put in him. I'd constantly believed he was on the verge
of doing the right thing . . . but I'd given him way too much
credit. I'd swallowed every reservation I'd had about entering
into this arrangement with him, but I couldn't do that anymore. I couldn't put my faith in something so shallow. And
that's what this was. A hollow, meaningless affair.

I rose to my feet and stood before him. "I deserve to be
more than just a wet hole to stick your . . ." I paused, fighting to
compose myself. "I'm more than just BFFs with your penis," I
blurted, unable to keep the raw emotion from my voice.

"Of course you are." He stood and smoothed his hands
up and down my upper arms. "What are you talking about?"

I shrugged away from his touch. His hands on my skin
wouldn't help me right now. I needed to be thinking clearly. I
needed to get some answers from him about where we stood.
I thought we'd been building to something more—starting
with him asking me to come on this trip with him—but
clearly we were no longer on the same page.

He crossed his arms over his chest and studied me objec-
tively, sizing me up. "Despite this arrangement, we're friends,
right?"

"Friends who fuck . . ." I clarified, my tone bitter and
harsh.

His jaw tightened. I sensed that he understood he was

digging himself into a deeper hole with every word. "What do you want, kitten?"

"I've never been to your apartment. We've never been out together on a date . . ." *And now you're hiding me in your hotel room like you're afraid of being seen with me, even though we're thousands of miles from home.*

He scrubbed his hands across his face. "I'm sorry. I should have known this would lead to real feelings. Fuck." He squeezed his eyes closed and pressed his fingers to his temples.

"I'm sorry this is so fucking hard for you to figure out, Braydon. Let me spell it out for you. I like you and I want more." I swallowed heavily, having laid myself bare. Adrenaline shot through my veins, warming me and making my hands shake. The ball was in his court. And that terrified me.

He looked down at the floor and licked his lips. "Nothing's changed for me. I told you from the beginning I wasn't looking for a girlfriend. I made that very clear. I thought I was honest with you . . ."

"You own me," I whispered, my voice broken and raspy.

"You think I don't know that? You think I don't see the way you look at me? I never meant for this to happen."

"For what?"

"Real feelings. You getting hurt. I feel like an asshole, Ellie."

"I'm sorry me falling for you is such a hardship for you." I wanted to say *loving* you, but I held my tongue. I couldn't say it. Couldn't put that out there when I knew I'd get so little in return.

"You don't understand my past." Angry hands tore through his hair. "Fuck, this is complicated. I just never wanted you to get hurt. I hope you believe that."

I didn't know what to believe anymore. I heaved a breath inward. Tears burned my vision, but I didn't want to break down in front of him. Our easygoing banter had left the building, and this moment was more real than any we'd had before. Maybe I'd misjudged everything. There wasn't anything real between us but sex. And I'd allowed myself to fall for him like a fucking moron. I crossed the room to the bathroom and closed the door behind me. The tears were coming, and there would be no stopping them.

Locking the bathroom door behind me, I pressed my hands against the cool marble surface of the countertop and hung my head. It had been a mistake to come here. I'd used up my hard-earned vacation time, spent two thousand dollars— my entire savings—on the airline ticket. I'd put everything on the line, had given myself to him completely, and what had I gotten in return? A body imprinted with the memory of sex with Braydon in every possible position so it'd be impossible to forget him.

I heard the hotel room door close with a thud. He had left. Just fucking fantastic. We weren't even going to discuss this like adults. I splashed cool water on my face, my sadness giving way to anger. Looking at my reflection in the mirror, I gave myself a much-needed pep talk. I decided then and there that I wouldn't allow myself to continue this arrangement. It wasn't healthy for me. *He* wasn't healthy for me. And if I wasn't going to continue this, I had no business in this hotel room with him. I considered for a moment going to Ben and Emmy's room, but knew that Braydon would come and find me and that all three of them would talk me into returning to his room. He had that power over me, to make me forget myself and give everything over to our shared chemistry. I couldn't allow that to happen. The only choice I had was to get the hell off this island.

I stormed from the bathroom, renewing my strength, and began hastily packing my suitcase. I would be gone before he came back from his walk, or wherever he'd gone. Screw him. I wasn't a doormat, and I wouldn't be used like one. I needed to get the fuck off this island.

11

One fact was undeniably clear: I was miserable without him. Like a fool, I'd powered on my phone after the long flight home, desperate to see missed calls, voice mails, or texts from him begging me to return, or promising me things would be different. But my phone was eerily quiet. Not a peep from him.

I'd sucked it up and returned to work, desperate for the distraction. I shot death glares at my boss and coworkers when they asked about my trip and why I was back early. *Because I decided to start thinking with my brain instead of my vagina for a change.*

Several days later, I heard from him. One lousy text. *I'm sorry I can't be who you want me to be.* Which I translated to mean that he wasn't even going to try. He could have fixed this all so easily between us if he really wanted to. Invite me over to his place, agree to meet up with me for coffee somewhere, tell me he was ready for more . . . but nope. He hadn't promised me a thing, and I was done grasping on to false hope and illusions for what would never be. The realization stung. I truly was just his bed buddy. The sex had been great, I wasn't about to lie to myself. It had been truly off the charts. He was the best lover I'd ever had—by far. That was the worst part of it all, because now I'd lost everything—no chance at love, and no more mind-blowing sex to take my mind off that fact. Fuck.

Worst of all, I felt like I'd lost a friend. Braydon and I had bickered nonstop when we'd first met. But it had all been in good fun. There was always an underlying electric current flowing between us—a spark. I'd felt so alive and care-free around him. He made me laugh easily and often. Those days were done. And even worse, he was best friends with my BFF's husband. There would be no way we could avoid each other forever. I guess I really should have thought that through before I started fucking him. Oh well. You live and you learn, I supposed.

I watched the calendar change days, throwing myself into routine. Work. Home. Gym. Laundry. It was all rather pathetic. I should have just let him go, wiped the slate clean, but I couldn't keep myself from looking at photos of him online. It started off innocently enough, with me checking Emmy's updates online. She posted photos of Ben regularly, like any good assistant would, from the various projects he booked. The latest were a series of shots from Hawaii. Deeply sensual poses of Ben and Braydon underneath a jungle waterfall with an exotic, fair-haired beauty between them. She appeared to be nude, just their hands covering her private areas, while they modeled a luxury line of men's swim trunks. My eyes zeroed in on Braydon. His expression was pure pleasure, primal and carnal. His look was so erotic, my sex muscles clenched, throbbing uncomfortably. My stupid vagina missed him. She'd gotten me into this mess in the first place. Well, no more, missy. *No soup for you!*

My stalking progressed from looking at photos from the Hawaii shoot into an hours-long obsession searching every last corner of the Internet for any trace of him, as if I could find something that would help me understand this man. I ate everything in sight, drank copious amounts of wine to help me sleep at night, and stalked him online, searching out every last picture while stuffing my face with pizza, cookie dough, and all the other foods I never let myself have. It was a full-on pity party for one.

True to his word, Braydon was usually photographed alone—he went sans date to most functions, occasionally escorting a fellow model. But as I tracked back in time, I realized things weren't always that way. The pictures that were a few years older showed him with a woman. She appeared on his arm during several events, and there were even candid shots of them together on the street. There was something familiar about her. And though her hair was darker in the pictures, I realized who it was. Katrina, the skittish girl I'd met at the photo shoot. I didn't know why it surprised me to see them together—she'd hinted at their history—but seeing his arms around her, the happy expressions on their faces . . . it was beyond strange. She seemed to be the one and only girl he'd been regularly photographed with.

I thought about his hesitation to be seen with me and I wondered if this woman, who he seemed all too happy to be photographed with, had anything to do with the sudden change.

Pulling my quilt up over my legs, I struggled to piece together the puzzle of Braydon. Maybe he had his heart broken and he was cautious about jumping into another relationship. Or maybe I was reading way too much into it and being way too generous. He could just be a player who acted on his baser instincts, like my subconscious first warned me about. He'd hinted at something in his past holding him back. Knowing I was no closer to solving the mystery, I did the only thing I could do. I went to grab the scrap of paper Katrina had given to me that was currently stuffed in my wallet. Maybe she held the key to his past, and maybe she could help me understand why he was the way he was.

Summoning my courage, I pulled the slip of paper from my wallet. Her neat, curvy handwriting covered the entire length of the scrap. I punched her number into my phone and typed out a text.

Me: Hey! It's Ellie from the photo shoot . . . remember me?

A few minutes later, her reply arrived.

Katrina: Hi! Of course I remember. How are you?

Me: Eh, I've been better. I was actually wondering if I could ask you a few Braydon-related questions . . . if that's not too strange.

My heartbeat thumped unevenly. I felt like a super-freak stalker. I hoped I didn't sound as pathetic as I felt. But something told me Katrina would be willing to share her experience.

Katrina: Oh no! What happened?

I couldn't tell if she was mocking me or genuinely interested in helping. If Braydon was single again, would that put her back in the running? I blew the strands of loose hair out of my face and plopped down on the couch. I had to try. She could help me piece together his past. And he'd cut me too deep. I had to know.

Me: I was tired of feeling like a plaything—I don't think he was ever really going to commit . . . so I sort of left him in Hawaii.

When I worded it like that, I sort of sounded like a bad-ass. I had put my foot down, it was true. I'd left him in a hotel and flown halfway across the globe. If I weren't feeling so utterly crappy, I might be proud.

Katrina: Dang, girl. How are you feeling now?

It was like she could sense that now that I was back home and all alone, the glow of pride in my decision had worn off. It was hard to feel proud when you were in sweatpants and a T-shirt and your heart felt like it'd been put through a blender.

Me: Basically like shit. ☺

The smiley face was pure sarcasm, but seriously, I didn't mean to be such a downer.

Katrina: Sorry. Been there. Done that. I understand. ☹

It was weird to think this stranger understood my situation better than anyone. Better than Emmy. But it would be nice to have someone to talk to about all this. I wondered if she still regularly Google-stalked Braydon. I wondered if a girl could ever really move on after someone like him. Probably not.

Me: I'm sure it sounds pathetic, but I was wondering if maybe you'd want to meet up for coffee or something . . . swap horror stories? It might help me to understand him better.

Katrina: It doesn't sound pathetic at all, and sure, I'd love to. You just let me know when you're up for it.

Me: Thanks. I will.

Heading back into my room, I felt the tiniest bit better. At least I had a plan. It might not have been the most noble of plans—to pump his ex-girlfriend for information—but hell, it was a start. I collapsed on my bed, curling into the sheets. There was no way not to notice that my pillowcase still smelled like him. I pulled the pillow to my face and inhaled deeply, letting his scent envelop me.

12

Several days later, Emmy and I sat at a sidewalk café, enjoying the fall sunshine and crisp air while we still could. I was so thankful she was back from her trip. Enduring this breakup alone had been torture. Especially since I knew my best friend was there with him, having fun in the sun, I was sure.

We sat over coffee and croissants as I poured my heart out to her. Once I'd finished, she lifted her chin, her eyes full of concern.

"You've fallen for him," she said with a frown. I nodded sheepishly. "Then why did you run?"

I bit my cheek. "Because I wasn't okay with being his dirty mistress. I wanted more."

She nodded sympathetically. "If it makes you feel any better, he was miserable once you left." I doubted that. But I avoided asking her if he found another girl on the island to replace me. I couldn't handle knowing that right now. "This is just like me and Ben in the beginning. We started out as just a fling. You told me not to chase him, remember? You said since he was used to women throwing themselves at him that I needed to be myself and show him that my appeal was that I was a regular girl. And if he liked me and wanted me in his life, he'd make it happen."

"That was my brilliant advice?" I cringed.

"Yes. And it worked. You were right then, and I'm right about this now. Braydon's used to the same thing, just like Ben was. Traveling the globe, dating supermodels, girls dropping their panties at a single flash of those dimples."

Shit, just picturing his adorable smile and dimples made my heart hurt. "Yes, and unfortunately I'm not a model, not even close, and I've already dropped my panties—two strikes against me. This will never work."

"Yes it will."

"None of this matters, Emmy. We're done. I left him in Hawaii and he hasn't even called."

"He will. Trust me."

I rolled my eyes. He had texted me once, but I didn't mention that to her. "And when he does, you need to distance yourself from him a bit. Let him miss you. He's already seen how great you are. You're smart, funny, sexy, and you give him a run for his money, too. I've never seen a girl keep up with Braydon's quips like you do. He's going to realize just how amazing that combination is. Just give him a little space to miss you."

I nodded. I knew she was right. What she was saying made sense. But the idea of distancing myself from him caused a physical ache to form in my chest.

"I've seen you guys together. You have amazing chemistry. I can only imagine what the sex is like between you two."

"Oh honey, you have no idea," I said with a chuckle. Emmy's cheeks grew the faintest bit pink. "He's fucking fantastic in bed. Seriously, I've never been with a man who knows the female body so well."

Emmy took a sip of her espresso. "Well, all that's got to be put on hold."

"Emmy, are you deaf? We're not even speaking. I certainly won't be sleeping with him anytime soon."

"Trust me, I know Braydon. He's going to call. So just promise me, when he does call, don't go to bed with him, missy. You need a hiatus to see what your relationship with him is really made of. And you need to make him work for it, despite how fabulous the sex is with him."

"It's more than just great sex. He's sweet, kind, funny, and so giving. He made me feel beautiful. And smart. He's the total package. You know, aside from that pesky detail of not wanting to be seen in public with me or have any type of real relationship." I faked a smile.

Emmy squeezed my hand from across the table. "Do you want me to have Ben say something to him?"

"God no. That would only make things awkward." I shuddered at the thought.

"He'll come to his senses." She sounded certain, but I had my doubts.

I shrugged. "We'll see. I'm not counting on it."

"I give him a week before he's begging for you to come back."

I scoffed, concentrating on my croissant, picking it into small pieces on my plate.

"Ells?"

I lifted my head. Oops, I guess I'd been lost in my own thoughts for a bit there.

"Just be careful. I don't want you to get hurt again."

I nodded. "I promise."

Regardless of the fact he probably wasn't going to call, I knew she was right. Maybe it was time to start dating again and renew my online dating profile, just to take my mind off of things with Braydon for a while.

Despite being back in town for several days, and Emmy's prediction that Braydon would contact me, he didn't. I tried not to be too crushed and went on with my life. It helped that I'd already had several interested guys emailing me, wanting to set up dates after I updated my online dating profile. I was just starting to feel better about things when Braydon took me by surprise on a Thursday night.

My phone rang, and as I went to pick it up, I saw Braydon's name flashing across the screen. I stood there in my kitchen, staring down at the phone like it was a ticking time bomb. It was a call. Not a text. I tried not to get my hopes up.

"Hello?" I finally answered.

"Hey," he said casually. If he was going to pretend like nothing was wrong—that our fight hadn't happened—I was going to lose it.

"I miss you," he said softly.

"I miss you, too," I blurted out before I could stop myself. *Shit*. So much for playing it cool and standing my ground. Did I have *any* self-respect left? Sheesh. I straightened my shoulders. "Braydon, why are you calling? You know where I stand."

"Yes, I do. You made that abundantly clear."

I waited, the gentle sound of his breathing and the faint humming of my refrigerator in the background the only sounds I could hear.

"I'm sorry I hurt you. I never meant for that to happen."

My heart kicked up a steady, thumping rhythm. "Go on."

"I thought we were on the same page with this arrangement . . . and I'm truly sorry about Hawaii. I'd like to see you," he said.

I didn't respond. I was trying to be strong. "Can I come over tomorrow night after work? We should probably talk," he said.

I wiped a stray tear from my cheek and inhaled deeply, needing to make sure my voice remained steady. "I have a date tomorrow night. Sorry."

"A date?" The surprise in his tone crashed through me. I wanted to feel proud, but instead I just felt shitty.

"Yeah. I figured it was time to, you know, take care of me and move on."

He didn't need to know my date was with a forty-year-old divorced guy I wasn't the least bit excited about. I was only going to force myself to try to move on.

"I see." His tone was soft, disappointed, and I fought with

myself to keep quiet. I wanted to tell him never mind, that I'd cancel my stupid date. But then I realized he was offering to come over. To my apartment. Not take me to his, not meet up in public. It was the same old, same old. That realization renewed my strength.

"Goodnight, Braydon."

"Night, kitten."

I sunk to the kitchen floor, pulling my knees up to my chest, and heaved deep, shuddering breaths as tears leaked from my eyes uncontrollably.

13

"Well?" Emmy asked, helping herself to another slice of pizza. "How was it?"

"How was what?"

"The date! Duh."

I rolled my eyes. I'd tried to block that from my memory. "Horrid. Ridiculous. Never happening again."

"Okay then." She stiffened. "Still, I'm proud of you for going. And most of all for putting Braydon in his place. Has he called again?"

I fought a wave of tears that threatened to escape. I couldn't help but wonder if I'd made a terrible mistake turning him down. I set my slice of pizza back on my plate. "No."

"Hang in there, babe."

It was easier said than done. I hadn't seen Braydon in more than three weeks. Sure, he'd been in Hawaii much of that time, but still, he'd had ample opportunity to miss me, hadn't he? And still, he hadn't called again.

• • •

In the weeks that followed, Emmy became increasingly busy with New York Fashion Week. In the position to be more selective about work that took him away from the charity, Ben wasn't walking in just any show. This made him even more in demand than usual, which Ben and Emmy used to their full advantage. Rather than simply being cast, they negotiated an exclusive appearance to the highest bidder. He'd chosen the Giorgio Armani show for a ridiculous sum that would go straight to his charity. I was proud of them for the careers they were building. It was cool to watch. They had the same vision and rarely disagreed, despite working long hours together.

Anytime Emmy brought up Fashion Week, I fought the urge to ask her about Braydon, which shows he was being cast in, and if he had any travel plans coming up. I knew that would only fuel my online-stalking of him. Fixating on him wasn't healthy. He'd clearly moved on and I needed to as well. I did agree to join Emmy and Ben at the Armani postshow soiree. Emmy had convinced me, saying that Ben would be busy chatting up the industry people and she would be left alone. I couldn't imagine a scenario in which Ben left his beautiful wife to fend for herself, but I agreed to go. Honestly, the party sounded like fun. It would give me an excuse to dress up, get out of my apartment, and mingle with pretty people. The idea that I might run into Braydon there only fueled my desire to attend.

He was still constantly on my mind, and even though I knew it wasn't healthy, I wanted to see him, I wanted him

to see me, and I wanted to find out if we still had any connection. That evening I spent an inordinate amount of time
blowing out my long hair with meticulous care until it was
a glossy mane that fell down my back in a silky curtain. He'd
take one look at me and drop down on his knees, begging for
me to come back. At least that's what I told myself as I got
ready for the night.

I'd had a facial and was pleased to see my skin was soft
and glowing. Applying my makeup was a breeze and I went
a little overboard, dusting bronzing powder across my forehead, along the bridge of my nose, and the tops of my breasts.
I added pink blush to the apples of my cheeks, berry lip gloss,
and two coats of black mascara. I felt sexy and confident when
I looked at the end result.

Without much time to fret over what I would say if I saw
him, I rushed to meet Emmy and Ben's driver outside my
building, grabbing my handbag and hustling down the stairs
to my awaiting chariot. It was kind of them to send Henry
for me. They'd both been tied up at different events all day,
working their connections to seek additional donors for their
charity, so I planned to meet them there.

I arrived at the swanky lounge where the afterparty was
being held and gave my name to the bouncer. The velvet
ropes were parted, allowing me to pass through. I felt very
posh strutting into the dimly lit space. And I had little choice
but to strut—my five-inch heels left me feeling like I was on
stilts.

Dozens upon dozens of little white candles dotted the

entire space and sheer white fabric floated down from the ceiling, tied into big bows that appeared to be suspended in midair. Pillows and cushions along the walls were the only seating and a large bar took up the entire back wall. I headed straight there, not sure what else to do with myself. Having a drink in hand would at least give me something to do.

Deciding to stick with the posh theme, I ordered a Cosmopolitan. Once I'd tipped the bartender, I accepted the martini glass and tasted the pink concoction. Potent but yummy. Turning from the bar, my eyes assessed the room. It was full of models and other industry people—publicists and photographers, I guessed. I spotted Ben across the room, chatting with an older man in a classic tux, but there was no sign of Emmy. And no Braydon, either. I concentrated on my drink once again. Parking myself on a barstool, I decided the little bowl of salted almonds would keep me company.

I dug my cell phone out of my little handbag to see if I'd missed a call from Emmy, but there was nothing. I considered texting her to find out where she was but decided I wouldn't bug her in case she was making some connection for their charity.

Within minutes I was ordering another Cosmo to replace the one I'd sucked down rather quickly. Geez, I could already feel the effects of the vodka and Triple Sec as the bartender placed the new drink in front of me. Across the room, I spotted a buffet table with delicious things to eat—sautéed shrimp on skewers, mini burgers and lettuce wraps, and, oh my God, was that cheesecake? The buffet was all but abandoned, but I wasn't going to let that stop me. These people were crazy—this mama needed to eat. And almonds and vodka hardly counted as dinner. Oh yes, I'd be hitting that up later.

After a few more sips, Emmy appeared beside me, beaming her megawatt smile in my direction. "You look amazing," she squealed, sizing me up. "I've never seen you wear that dress. Very sexy," she nodded.

"Thank you." I didn't mention it was a new ensemble I'd bought just for this event on the small chance that I'd run into Braydon. It had cost me a fortune, but I didn't care. I had to look my best; it was practically in the *Dealing with Your Ex* handbook. I smoothed the wine-colored stretchy fabric over my hips and smiled at my wardrobe choice. The dress left very little to the imagination. It hugged all my curves and displayed the girls nicely—the top of the dress draping down rather dramatically to showcase my décolletage and ample cleavage. It was a little more—okay a lot more—than I'd normally show off, but hell, it was a special occasion. It wasn't every day I got invited to an Armani fashion show afterparty. The back of the dress also fell away to reveal my lower back, and the gray suede pumps were the perfect complement to my ensemble.

"How's everything going? How was the show?" I asked, taking another gulp of my beverage. It was going to go straight to my head, but, damn, this thing was good.

I listened while Emmy filled me in on their day, that everything had gone great—and just when I was working up the courage to ask if she'd seen Braydon, she beat me to it:

"And I thought we'd run into Bray. He was in a bunch of shows today; I heard he opened the Calvin Klein show in a pair of briefs, sexy nerd glasses, boots, and a scarf," she said with a laugh. "But I haven't seen him anywhere." She said something about the emphasis of the show being on men's accessories, but I tuned her out and daydreamed about Braydon strutting down a catwalk in a pair of nut-hugging briefs. Mother, that would have been a sight to see. The Calvin Klein show would surely be up on YouTube . . . I knew what I was doing later. In fact, I wondered if it'd be possible to sneak into a corner unnoticed and look it up now on my smartphone. No, best to wait for tonight, when I could provide myself some relief.

Emmy rattled on about some snafu behind the scenes while guys were changing and an overzealous photographer rudely tried to sneak in a shot, when suddenly I felt the air around me shift. A warm current zipped along my spine and the hair on the back of my neck tingled. I spun around and spotted Braydon across the room.

He was facing me, but hadn't seen me yet. Probably because he was engaged in what looked like a riveting conversation with a woman. His eyes crinkled with mischief and his crooked smile beckoned her on. Her back was to me, but I could only imagine she was a model. I cataloged our differences. Where she was sharp angles and thin legs poking beneath her dress, I was soft curves and rounded flesh filling out mine. I felt inadequate. But rather than studying her, my eyes fell back to him.

Emmy's voice quieted, realizing what had captured my attention. "Oh," she mumbled.

He tossed the girl in front of him a crooked smile and my heart tripped over itself, knowing just how it felt to be treated to that beautiful, dimpled grin. God, just being near him was brutal. I wanted to rush to him, throw my arms around his waist, nestle in against his chest, push my fingers into his messy hair, and kiss his full mouth, which I knew was soft yet demanding at the same time.

My eyes slid down his body and a current pulsed through me. My gaze fell from his face to his broad chest, down to his long muscular thighs covered in dark slacks. I caught movement and dropping my eyes lower, I caught the faceless blonde with her hand over the front of his dress pants. She was toying with his belt buckle rather suggestively while balancing on tiptoes to whisper something near his ear. Her manicured hand continued caressing his manhood. I felt bitter acid rise up my throat in protest.

Emmy's sharp intake of breath signaled she'd spotted the rather noticeably indecent display as well. It had been a terrible idea to come here. This was his world, and I wasn't a part of it anymore. I never had been. He'd clearly moved on. I hadn't. Not one bit. My heart ached for him. And my stomach churned violently in response to seeing him with another woman. I needed to leave. I rose from my seat on shaky legs and turned toward the exit.

Braydon's eyes latched on to mine and everything we'd

previously shared slammed into me with ferocious force. I locked my knees, fighting to remain steady in the too-high heels.

I dropped my gaze to the floor and mumbled something to Emmy about it being no big deal. A complete lie, of course. I felt desperate and sick, my stomach filled with acid.

His eyes burned into mine as if to inquire how badly he'd fucked things up with me. My mouth remained relaxed as I fought for control. I wouldn't release the venom I so desperately wanted to, which would let him know just how hard this was for me. Before I had time to figure out my strategy, Braydon was just steps away, his eyes still locked on mine like a cheetah stalking its prey.

My stomach tightened into a knot. I knew I wasn't strong enough for him to make some smart quip and joke about what we'd shared. I'd lose it completely if he was just going to downplay what we'd had. But as he approached, his face turned serious, his jaw tight with tension. He looked troubled.

Tears swam in my eyes. Tears I couldn't let him see. The door was twenty feet away. So close yet also way too far. I had to make it. I needed the freedom, the fresh air, a Braydon-free zone. Just as I was starting for the door, a firm hand caught my wrist and spun me to face him.

"Talk to me, kitten."

Unable to meet his blue eyes, my head dropped down. His erection had slackened. *God, why was I even looking at that?*

"No need—you can go back to your date." I flicked my free hand in the direction of the hussy across the bar. "I shouldn't have come here."

Anger seethed just below the surface and Braydon sucked in a sharp breath. "But you did. Now tell me why."

I scoffed. "I don't owe you anything, Braydon."

His hand tightened around my wrist—not enough to hurt, but enough to know that he wasn't letting me go without a fight.

If he wanted a fight, I'd give it to him. I'd fled paradise without really explaining myself, and if he wanted the truth, I'd let him have it.

His tone softened. "For the record, I'm not here with anyone. Are you mad at me?"

I shook my head, thinking it over. "More like mad at myself."

"For?" he asked, dark brows drawing together.

"For allowing myself to get too close to you. That arrangement wasn't healthy for me."

He thought it over, his jaw working. "I'm sorry. I thought having boundaries in place would make it easier for you. I tried to be honest from the start about what I was looking for."

"And you were. It just turned out that I couldn't do it."

"That's not how I remember it." His tone had dropped lower and his eyes were still serious, still pinned on mine.

"W-what do you mean?" I stammered, heat suddenly rising to my cheeks.

"When you let yourself be free—when you stopped fighting it—you enjoyed yourself. Immensely."

I swallowed a gulp of air as memories of Braydon flooded my system. His lips at my throat, him moving above me, me down on my knees, lightly rubbing my tongue along the steel barbell piercing while he groaned in pleasure. I wanted to argue with him, to tell him off, but instead I stood there gutted by his words, by his honest assessment of me. He always saw more than I wanted him to. "I'm not going to deny that. We both know this chemistry between us is . . ."

"Off the charts," he finished for me.

I nodded. "But that's not everything, Braydon. I was looking for a connection, the promise of something more—if not right away, maybe later down the line. But that possibility never manifested between us. I never got that from you."

He remained silent, his eyes locked on mine. He couldn't argue. Releasing a deep sigh, his hand found mine and he laced our fingers together. "I've missed you," he admitted softly.

Damn it. My pulse rioted. My body remembered everything.

Braydon's gaze lowered, moving down my curves, which suddenly felt much too exposed. "What the fuck is this dress?"

"You don't like it?"

"I didn't say that . . . but it will be a little difficult walking around all night with an erection."

I laughed. I couldn't help myself. Oh my God, it had been weeks since I'd actually laughed. That felt damn good. Better than I remembered. The tension I'd been carrying in my shoulders eased and I instantly felt calmed.

His hands smoothed over my hips. "Seriously, baby, a bathing suit would have been less revealing. Fuck."

I relished his compliments and the lust-filled look in his eyes despite myself. I knew Braydon and I weren't finished. Not by a long shot. He still yearned for me as much as I did for him. Only now I had to decide if I was ready to jump back in. My brain was screaming no and my body was crying yes.

He leaned down, brushing his lips past my neck, making me gasp at the sudden rush of hot breath against my skin. "We need to talk."

I nodded. I needed to hear what he had to say.

Taking my hand, he led me down a hallway off the side of the banquet room. We continued down the hall, passing by the restrooms until we reached a door labeled "Office." Braydon tried the doorknob, his other hand still gripping mine. The office was dark and empty. Braydon flipped on the light and closed the door behind us. It was a small square room with no window, just a single desk and chair in the center of the room facing the door.

He'd taken my hand hostage and seemed reluctant to let it go. God, I'd missed his touch even more than I realized. My blood simmered any time our skin made contact. I needed a moment to just breathe. Crossing the room, I ran my finger over the top of the desk, stalling for time. What was there to say?

Braydon stalked toward me, his eyes once again caressing my curves and making me feel all but naked. I took a step back. This room was way too small and suddenly much too warm.

"You left me," he murmured.

I remained silent. There was no sense in arguing. I had left him without any explanation.

"I thought you'd gone for a drink or something at first, but then I noticed your suitcase was gone. I called Emmy and she didn't know a thing."

I hadn't even messaged Emmy to tell her I was back in New York until the following morning. I didn't want to be talked into staying.

His fingertip traced my hip bone in the most distracting way. "Did I not give you what you needed?" he whispered.

"In the bedroom, yes. But outside of it, no. I needed more, a lot more." I wasn't going to deny that any longer.

"I see." He dropped his hand from my waist and the absence of his touch left me bereft, wanting. "I've missed you, if that counts for anything."

It did. I heaved a breath inward. God, I shouldn't have drunk all those Cosmos. I felt slightly dizzy and a lot horny. Bad combination around this man. I knew it would only lead to trouble. Trouble I very much wanted. "I've missed you, too," I admitted in a moment of weakness.

"But you're the one who ended it." His brows pinched together.

My eyes acknowledged his statement, dropping to the floor briefly, as if to say, *I know*. Being near him, inhaling him, was a deadly combination. My body was responding to the maleness of his scent, my heartbeat ricocheting off the walls of my chest, making my breath come out in soft pants.

"You're sending me all kinds of mixed signals, kitten." His eyes fell to my chest where my nipples had hardened into pebbles. I dropped my head, but his index finger lifted my chin until I met his eyes once again. "You have no idea how badly I've missed you," he growled, lightly nipping at my neck. "Let me show you. Let me make it up to you . . ." I released a soft groan. "I need to be inside you."

"Not here," I moaned.

His eyes rose to mine. "Your place. We'll grab a cab."

I nodded my consent and he grabbed my hand to tow me from the office; we weaved our way through the throngs of mingling bodies when I stopped suddenly. "Wait . . ."

He stopped suddenly. "What?"

I looked longingly at the buffet table. "I didn't get to try any of the yummy things over there. . . ."

He chuckled beside me, his posture immediately relaxing. "Give me one sec." He kissed my cheek and then rushed over to the tuxedo-clad attendant restocking napkins at the buffet. Within minutes he was handed a large brown paper bag that I could only assume was filled with to-go treats. My hero.

My smile widened as he approached, the bag clutched in his hands. "Now we're ready. No more stalling." He grabbed my hand and all but hauled me out the door.

Once we reached my apartment, Braydon gathered the plates and silverware from the kitchen while I unpacked the sack of treats on my small dining table. We ate and laughed and caught up about the past several weeks, avoiding any heavy topics. It was crazy how easily we could fall back into our old routine. I knew there was a big conversation we still needed to have—about where we stood—but even I seemed reluctant to start it. This felt too good and I wasn't ready to ruin it.

"Are you going to finish that slice of cheesecake?" He looked longingly at my plate.

"Every last bite," I confirmed, grinning wickedly as I shoved a big piece of the cake into my mouth. "But . . ." I pulled the last container from the bag. "There's another slice, and I'll split it with you if you make coffee."

"Deal."

I loved that I could be myself with him. I'd forgotten how easy we were together. Like two old friends who taunted and teased each other endlessly, and of course had great sex, too. My stomach flipped at the thought. I wouldn't be giving in to him tonight. Couldn't.

After our meal, we washed the dishes and then settled in the living room. The conversation soon died down and a comfortable silence settled in around us. A steaming mug of coffee, a belly full of cheesecake, and Braydon back in my life. Things were good. Maybe we could do this—even if it was just as friends. Things felt too natural, too easy with him, and I didn't want to lose that.

Braydon pushed my hair back behind my shoulder. "Come here. I don't bite."

I glared at him, but moved closer. I knew in fact he did bite.

Although I had removed my killer heels, I hadn't yet changed out of my dress. And my body suddenly realized that only a thin scrap of fabric was separating Braydon's skin from mine.

"I'm going to go change out of my dress," I informed him, hopping up from the couch.

"Need a hand?" he asked, rising.

"No." I pushed his shoulders so he returned to sitting. "Sit. Stay. Good puppy." I patted his head.

He lifted a dark sexy brow at me.

"Boys are like puppies," I explained. "You have to have lots of patience, plenty of discipline, house-train them . . ."

"Is that so?"

I nodded, feeling satisfied.

"Does that mean girls are like kittens? Give them lots of snuggles and give them cream to lick up so they don't get ornery and claw you?"

I giggled. "Something like that. Be right back."

Once inside my bedroom, I didn't bother with closing the door. I heard the television flip on and figured Braydon was making himself comfortable.

I unzipped my dress and stepped out of it, crossing the room in bare feet to hang my dress in the closet. I was humming the tune from the commercial I could hear coming from the living room and spun around to a rich grumble. Braydon was watching me from the doorway. I sucked in a breath as our eyes locked.

He remained motionless in the door, his dark blue eyes possessive and hungry.

"What are you doing?" My voice came in a rush of breath.

"Take off your bra."

What?

His gaze dropped to the swell of generous cleavage that spilled over my pink push-up bra.

My body obeyed his command, my traitorous hands finding the clasp behind my back and releasing it. I let the straps fall from my shoulders, but palmed the cups of the bra before I was left completely exposed.

Braydon crossed the room and lightly gripped my wrists. "Don't hide from me. I don't know where this is headed, but this thing between us is real. I know you feel it, too."

My brain latched on to his statement that he didn't know where this was headed—wouldn't make me any promises, but he was right, I felt more for him than I had for anyone in a long, long time. And not to mention, my body was humming for his touch. It had been so long, and no one knew my body quite like Braydon. I craved him. Even though I knew he was bad for me. "We shouldn't," I murmured, finding my voice.

"Don't you think I know that? I don't mean to mess with you like this—I never meant for things to get so complicated. But I want you. I want your friendship, and fuck, I want this body too, if you'll let me have you."

I chewed on my lower lip, weighing his words.

Braydon gently tugged my wrists away and my bra fell to the floor.

He inhaled sharply and cursed under his breath. He cupped my naked breasts, his thumbs lightly grazing my nipples. Darts of pleasure shot through me, sending a rush of warmth to my core.

Braydon watched my reaction with interest, his dark eyes missing nothing—not the rosy blush that was crawling up my neck or the way my breathing came in soft pants. He lowered his head and with his eyes still locked on mine, he pressed a tender kiss to the top of one breast, then the other. I ached to feel his mouth against my sensitive nipples and he didn't deny me. His hot mouth closed over a nipple, his wet tongue loving it with soft strokes. A cry broke from my lips and my knees trembled. His hands pressed the weight of my breasts together and his mouth moved from one to the other, licking, sucking, and biting gently all while I writhed against his talented mouth.

Braydon pulled away, rising to meet my lips. He pressed a tender kiss to my mouth, then rubbed his thumb along my lower lip. The dampness he'd left behind on my breasts puckered my nipples in the cool air. He looked me over, his blue eyes alive with arousal and his slacks heavily tented in the front.

Not expecting anyone to see my panties tonight, I had on a pair of comfy black boy shorts. But the way his hands found my ass cheeks, which peeked from the bottom, he didn't seem to mind in the least. He knew how to turn me on until I was soaking wet and nearly ready to beg. His fingers toyed with the waistband of my panties, dipping barely inside with featherlight touches to tease and arouse. The skin on my hips and stomach broke out in chill bumps. I rubbed a hand over the front of his pants, feeling his fully erect manhood, and my sex muscles clenched.

"Can I have you tonight?" he asked, breathless.

My brain was screaming at me to give in, to rip my panties down my legs and undo his pants . . . but my heart was throbbing painfully, reminding me of the ache only he could produce. "Have you been with anyone else?" I held my breath.

He shook his head. "No. There's no one else."

My breath whooshed past my lips as I breathed a sigh of relief. "Are you staying the night?" Cuddling with him was my favorite postsex activity. Sleeping warm and secure in Braydon's arms made everything okay.

"Of course. After I orgasm, I can pretty much crash anywhere." He chuckled lightly, looking at me like this was a fact I should know about him by now.

So not what I wanted to hear. I drew a deep breath and took a step back from him. Despite how sweet and attentive he was with me, that was still all this was. He made that crystal clear. This was sex between two consenting adults. Plain and simple. I could take it, or I could leave it. I knew exactly what I needed to do.

I crossed the room and stood at my open bedroom door. "Good-bye, Braydon."

He adjusted his erection and came to stand next to me, pressing his palm against my cheek. "Kitten?"

"This has got to be fifty-fifty. If you can't give me what I need, I won't give you what you want."

"What are you saying?" His thumb lightly rubbed my cheek.

"This isn't going to work for me."

Sad blue eyes met mine. "Understood."

I wanted him to argue, to fight for me, but I knew that wouldn't happen. Even more of a reason to let him go.

As I watched him pull his shirt back on over his head, my heart ached painfully in my chest, fearing that this was it. I wondered if this was the last time I would see him.

Without even a last glance my way, Braydon left me in my too-quiet apartment. Naked and alone.

14

Emmy came over a few evenings later to check in on me after my disastrous night with Braydon. We'd just finished giant spinach salads and garlic rolls from the deli downstairs and were sitting cross-legged on my living room floor, casually chatting about life, work, and any other topic that wasn't my cringe-worthy love life. Thank God.

Never had I felt so out of control, so powerless around a man. Sometimes it infuriated me the way Braydon made me feel. Other times it was so completely blissful that it made my entire life's outlook brighter. Today was not one of those days. I used to be so fearless giving Emmy advice when it came to Ben. I'd tell her not to take any shit. To not give into his sexual advances—to make him sweat a little. It was so easy from the sidelines. I wasn't emotionally involved.

Things with Braydon were so much more complicated. I'd inadvertently given him not only my body but also my heart. I knew deep down I was falling for him. I'd fallen for his quick wit and sense of humor, for his sexy confidence, for the way he made me feel about myself. Aside from his commitment issues, he was sweet, a true gentleman. It was dangerous territory, especially because I was damn certain this was all just physical for him. He'd reminded me time and again.

"Sooo," Emmy began, a hint of concern on her face. "Are we going to talk about it?"

I shrugged. "What's there to talk about? I caved last weekend—brought him home with me." It was a low point; that was for certain. It wouldn't be happening again.

"And what happened? I know you two aren't back together, so . . . tell me what happened that night. You better spill it, little miss. You know there's no holding back from me."

I swallowed my pride. "We started to . . . you know . . ." I wiggled my eyebrows—the universal signal for getting it on. "And then I realized that nothing had changed, I was still nothing more to him than his fuck buddy, and I lost it. I kicked him out of my apartment with a raging erection." And then cried myself to sleep.

"Wow. You don't fuck around. I like it, lady."

I frowned at her. This wasn't some game—not for me, anyway. I wasn't trying to whip Braydon into shape. I just couldn't put myself through the heartache again, so I ended it before it went too far.

"Well, don't you worry, babe. I know he's crazy about you. He's going to come around."

She sounded so confident, but I was pretty sure there

was no chance of that. I'd given him every opportunity in the world.

"Let me ask you something . . ."

I explained about the insight I'd developed while stalking him online—and how I rarely saw him pictured with a girl—except for the one blond-haired girl, Katrina, though I didn't tell Emmy I knew her. "Did he ever have a serious girlfriend?" I asked.

"I think so. A few years ago. Ben said something about how he'd gotten royally messed up when it ended and he's really leery about new relationships and letting people in because of a crazy girl he dated a few years ago. That's all I know."

"Do you know her name?"

Emmy shook her head. "Let me see the pictures you found."

I agreed, grabbing my laptop from the counter and logging in. At the first click of my mouse, I knew it was a terrible idea. His face appeared and my heart throbbed painfully in my chest. I missed him. Terribly. That chiseled jawline, his full mouth that used to erupt into a crooked smile with one simple quip. His insanely blue eyes fringed in dark lashes, the rumpled mess of dark hair. Seeing him on my screen wasn't enough. It didn't even compare to the real thing. I wanted to press my face into his neck and inhale, wrap my arms around his firm body, feel his gentle caress on my skin, hear the sweet words he would murmur.

Emmy studied each photo along with me, but found nothing even remotely familiar about the girl featured with him.

"So how do you feel?" she asked, nodding once toward my computer screen.

I sighed and thought it over. "I miss him. Too fucking much. And it makes me want to do strange things . . ." I rubbed my temples.

"Like?"

"I want to cook for him, do his laundry, fold his boxers into neat little squares. Something is majorly wrong with me."

Her expression softened. "Oh honey. You love him."

"Nooo. That's not it. I've read studies about this. It's just pheromones. Like some strange chemical reaction that my body has to his. Some people can have this unexplained attraction. Braydon and I obviously have it. That's all this is. It doesn't mean we'd even be capable of having a lasting, loving relationship." I remained objective in my assessment, grasping on to the science of it.

"Really?" She cocked an arched eyebrow. "And wanting to do a man's laundry doesn't tip you off that maybe your feelings go a bit deeper than that?"

No, my feelings couldn't extend beyond the bedroom. I couldn't love him, that wasn't part of the arrangement. My heart just needed to get the memo.

The following day, in a moment of weakness, I texted Katrina again.

Me: Hey! Are you up for meeting for coffee today?

Several minutes later, she replied.

Katrina: I'm busy today, but how about a drink tonight?

Me: Sounds great.

Once we'd set the time and place, I instantly felt calmed. Maybe tonight I'd get some answers about Braydon's past.

When I arrived, I spotted Katrina right away. Her shiny blond hair was curled in tight ringlets that fell around her shoulders. She was dressed in skinny jeans with a cute top and matching scarf and large dangling earrings. She looked nice, even if she was trying a little too hard. My own hair was in a ponytail and I'd opted for comfort—jeans and a long-sleeved T-shirt.

She hopped down off her barstool as I approached and gave me a hug like she was holding on for dear life. Maybe our shared experiences had bonded us more than I knew. Something told me I was about to find out.

We ordered our cocktails—she a glass of wine and me a Shirley Temple because I had to work in the morning and was tired of feeling like crap when I woke up. Once our beverages arrived, we sipped them in silence for several moments while I figured out what to say.

"So . . . how are you doing?" she asked, concern reflecting from her misty blue eyes.

I shrugged. "Not great. I still miss him."

"Have you seen him?"

"Yes, we've seen each other, but nothing's changed since I walked out on him in Hawaii. He's still the same old Braydon with his issues."

She nodded, knowingly. "Yeah, he's tough to pin down. It's okay to miss him." The faraway look in her eyes made me wonder if she was talking to me or more to herself with that comment.

"So tell me more about your history with him—if you're comfortable sharing," I added.

"Yeah, I'm an open book. We dated for nine months. The best nine months of my life. We traveled abroad, went hiking in Belize, surfing in Thailand, dined in five-star restaurants, attended red carpet events. It was a fairy tale. I thought he was it for me—I'd found my forever. My parents were so happy for me. They wanted to meet him. But they never got that chance." Katrina clamped her lips shut and the misty look in her eyes made me wonder if I'd hear any more. I wanted to know why they broke up—what had happened to end their fairy-tale romance to make Braydon into the jaded man he was today.

As silly as it was, something else was still bugging me. "Can I ask you a question?"

She nodded.

"When you were together, you went to his apartment, right? I don't know why it bugs me, but I don't even know where he lives."

"Yes," she confirmed. "I stayed with him most weekends. But he moved a few months after we broke up and I don't know where he lives now."

"Oh." I guess that would stay a mystery.

Katrina straightened her shoulders and kept the topic

light. She told story after story about their dating history—the places they'd been, things they'd done—recalling funny things he'd said, often making herself erupt in laughter. It all struck me as very sad. Their relationship had ended two years ago and she hadn't moved on. Not one bit. My stomach churned. I couldn't be like this girl. Realization struck me smack in the face. Maybe I already was.

A short time later, we said our good-byes, Katrina making me promise I'd keep her updated on what happened with Braydon, and I agreed.

If anything, my meeting with her strengthened my resolve about Braydon. I needed all or nothing. Seeing how she was still very much hung up on him was almost too painful to watch. I vowed not to become her.

15

A new project at work had left me blissfully busy and was almost enough to distract me from constantly thinking about Braydon. But now it was the weekend and my sorry ass couldn't stop picturing his pretty blue eyes and messy dark hair or remembering the way his strong arms felt around me. That was why his text on Saturday afternoon totally took me by surprise. It was like he'd somehow known I was sitting here, pining for him.

Braydon: Hiya kitten

Me: Hello

Braydon: I miss you.

Me: Me too.

Braydon: I hate how we left things.

Me: I know. ☹

Braydon: I get that our arrangement didn't work for you, but the worst part is, I feel like I lost a friend.

It was true, I felt the exact same way. I missed having him in my life. And stalking his photo shoots online wasn't enough. I had no clue what to say. He knew how I felt. He'd either reciprocate or he wouldn't.

Braydon: I was wondering if you'd meet me for coffee?

Wow. I had to reread the text twice. He'd never asked me for coffee before.

Me: Sure. That'd be nice. ;)

Braydon: Cool. You free now?

Interesting. Braydon Kincaid missed me and wanted to see me in a casual setting. Progress? My day was suddenly looking up. It was crazy how a bit of attention from this man could change my entire outlook. I was addicted to him.

He suggested a little café that he said was quiet and out of the way, about halfway between his place and mine. I still didn't know where he lived, but now I supposed I had a clue.

An hour later we were seated at a small round table with steaming mugs of coffee in front of us, an awkward silence big enough to fill a stadium settling between us. I didn't know what to say, he didn't know where to look.

"So . . . we're out . . ." I raised my eyebrows, glancing around the room.

While we were out in public, Braydon was right, this coffee shop was a hole in the wall, a teeny tiny place tucked between a couple of office buildings. In fact, there was only one other patron inside. Suddenly I was seeing our first outing with new eyes. And I wasn't happy.

I set down my coffee and planted my elbows on the table. "Listen, I get that you're embarrassed to be seen with me. I know I'm no supermodel, but shit, this is kind of a blow to the ego."

Braydon leaned forward. "No, that's not it at all. It's complicated."

I waited for him to say more, but he remained utterly silent. "Okay. Bye." I stood and grabbed my purse from the back of the chair. *Complicated, my ass.* I wasn't going to sit here in this dump and pretend it was a date any more than I was going to pretend a polished turd was a Tootsie Roll.

"Ellie, wait." He rose and clutched my hand, preventing my escape. "I'm sorry. Listen, I'll explain it."

He guided me back to my seat and I sat, but I kept my purse clutched in my lap.

"Shit, where do I start?" He rubbed a hand through his disheveled hair.

I bit my lip, waiting.

"There was this girl . . ."

Ah, it always started off with a girl. I hated that someone who had come before me had messed with his head so badly, but I suspended judgment and just listened. He was finally talking and opening up. Maybe this was a start.

"We dated for a while and things were fine. But once it was over, she turned ultraclingy and crazy. She began stalking me. She'd show up everywhere, at my work, my apartment, you name it. Calling nonstop, crying, begging for me back. It got really out of hand and it actually got so bad, I had to get a restraining order against her."

"Wow."

"I wrecked my last girlfriend. She went on antidepressants, suicide watch, and had to move back in with her parents."

That was not what I was expecting. I continued listening while our coffee grew cold as he told me the whole sordid tale.

"It's been really hard for me to date because she would follow me. And as far as pictures with women I was seeing, I tried to limit them so that she wouldn't target them. She would look them up online and start harassing them, too, trying to get information about me."

"Well, that's either the most elaborate story for ensuring you stay single or your ex is one crazy bitch," I said, finally.

"It's not a story. I wish it was. As much as it might surprise you, I like being in a relationship. I like having a girlfriend, cooking together, cuddling in bed all day, watching movies. I'm a regular guy, not some commitment-phobic asshole, I swear."

I wasn't sure why, but I believed him. But that didn't mean his past sat well with me. We talked for a few minutes more, but I feared we were at some kind of impasse. With Braydon unwilling or unable to move forward, and me insisting that I needed all or nothing, I worried about what this all meant.

As much as I'd appreciated finally hearing the truth from

him, it hadn't changed where we stood. He might have clued me in about what was going on, but he hadn't opened up his life or asked me to be part of it.

We parted ways in the street with a friendly hug and then he was gone, leaving me wondering about how we were leaving things. Again.

16

That Friday night, I fretted over what to wear. Ben and Emmy were having a little housewarming party for their newly renovated, postflood place together, and I knew Braydon would be there. We'd texted each other off and on over the past week about how our workdays had been, a new restaurant he discovered, trivial things like that. But we had avoided all serious topics. This would be the first time I'd seen him since he opened up to me. I wondered what the night would bring.

I chose a pair of black skinny jeans with knee-high boots and a soft gray sweater that clung to my best assets. Casual yet cute. Emmy had rejected my numerous offers for helping with the party, but I refused to arrive empty-handed, so I stopped on the way over and picked up a giant bouquet of fresh flowers for her. The hostess could never have too many flowers, right?

I was one of the first to arrive and Emmy was still setting up, so I jumped into action beside her in the kitchen. "Where do you need me?"

She gave a quick glance around the kitchen and pointed at a pile of lemons and limes on the counter. "Slice those into wedges for drink garnishes, please!"

"You got it." I grabbed a knife and cutting board and went to work. Soon we had everything under control, guests began filtering in, and we started setting out cheeses, fruits, and other yummy bite-sized treats, along with plenty of refreshing cocktails. The large arrangement of flowers I'd brought looked perfect in the cut-crystal vase in the center of Emmy's new dining table.

Helping set up for the party provided a great distraction. But soon the air around me changed and I realized Braydon had arrived. He stood in the center of the living room talking with a tall thin blonde with tits the size of Texas. Just great. Who the hell invited Buxom Barbie?

"That's Marissa," Emmy leaned in and whispered to me. I shrugged. I shouldn't care.

"She's a makeup artist Ben's worked with several times. Probably Bray, too. Don't look so worried." She bumped her hip into mine, trying to lighten my mood.

It didn't help. I dumped a bag of pretzels into a bowl and shoved it at her. "It doesn't matter, Em. Just drop it." *Shit.* My hands trembled as I moved on to my next task—refilling the ice. Maybe it had been a mistake to come here. When my eyes lifted to Braydon again, he was alone this time. And watching me.

"You're not even going to come say hi?" he teased, smiling crookedly at me from across the room.

"Sorry, I thought you were busy," I called out. *Busy with Slutty Barbie.*

"Come here." He opened his arms and I immediately went to him, folding myself into his embrace. His strong arms closed around me and I inhaled against his chest.

"How have you been?" The brightness in his eyes and the sincerity in his voice took me by surprise.

I shrugged. "Okay, I guess."

His jaw tensed. He looked like he wanted to say something more, but I got called away by Emmy to help with removing the appetizers from the oven.

She thrust a pair of oven mitts at me. "Sorry. I thought you needed saving."

I shook my head. "No, he was . . ." I searched for the right word. . . .

"He's sweet with you," Emmy observed, watching Braydon with a look of admiration.

Yeah, real sweet. He didn't want to be seen in public with me, and in private he commanded my body and my heart like no one else. A real sweetie. I removed the crab wontons from the oven and began plating them, thankful for the distraction.

I avoided the chance to mingle by staying in the kitchen. I liked this role. It allowed Emmy to spend time with her guests while I kept the snacks refilled and cleared away empty plates, all while sipping my wine in peace and watching Braydon discuss sports, politics, and modeling with various guests throughout the room. I had the perfect vantage point. God, his butt was cute in those jeans. Refilling my own wineglass yet again, I settled onto a barstool at the kitchen island. I'd probably been a little too liberal with my own wine consumption, but what the hell. I was at the housewarming party for two of my married, very in-love friends and was face-to-face with my ex-fuck friend. Yay, me.

Suddenly realizing Braydon was standing just two feet away, looking concerned, I lowered the glass from my lips. I wasn't sure when he'd entered the kitchen or how long he'd been staring at me, but he stepped closer and brought a hand to my jaw. He dragged his thumb across my damp lower lip, wiping away a trace of red wine. "You're frowning."

I swallowed. Hard. Then forced a smile.

"Why are you sad?" he asked.

"I'm fine, Braydon. Really."

He narrowed his eyes. "Kitten . . ." His tone was cocksure and imploring. I pulled in a shuddering breath and he dropped his hand, lacing his fingers behind his head. "I thought about what you said, and I realized I wasn't being fair to you."

"Go on." My heart kicked up a steady thumping rhythm.

"I told you when we agreed to this arrangement that I'd take care of you. And I failed at that. I didn't take care of all your needs as I should have."

"What are you saying?"

"You needed more," he said simply.

"Yes, I did," I murmured.

"I've thought about it, and I don't want to lose what we had, so . . ." He hesitated briefly. "I'm going to try and give you a bit more."

"What do you mean?" Either I'd consumed far too much wine or he was speaking in code.

"I'm asking you out."

"Out?"

"Yes, out. Will you join me for dinner tomorrow night?"

"Like at a restaurant? In public?"

"That's the plan."

I'd done what Emmy had said, put distance between us, let him miss me, and apparently it had worked. I wanted to jump up and down and do some air-humping right there in the kitchen, but instead I remained composed. "Um, sure. Why not?"

He chuckled at me. "Cool."

Wow. This was quite the one-eighty. My stomach flipped as I realized what this meant. I wasn't alone in my feelings for him. He wanted me back. Maybe he would come around after all, open himself up to me like I wanted. Remembering Emmy's advice, I took a deep breath, preparing myself to turn him down, even though I wanted to go running straight back into his arms. "Oh, actually, I would love to but I'm getting together with Emmy. I'm free on Sunday."

"Sunday's perfect. I'll pick you up at seven."

"Okay. And Braydon?"

"Yeah."

"Thanks."

"See you soon, kitten."

Emmy burst through the kitchen door just as Braydon was returning to the party. "Tell me everything," she demanded, hopping up and down.

I blew out a sigh. Was he asking me out because he genuinely wanted to date me, or because he'd promised me that all my needs would be met when I'd agreed to his arrangement? I would need Emmy to help me try and decipher the latest in my ongoing saga with Braydon Kincaid. "We're going on a date."

She squealed and pulled me in for a hug.

The night of our date arrived and Braydon called to warn me when he was coming over to my place. I met him downstairs, where he had a cab waiting. He gave me a warm hug, pressing his body to mine, and I almost collapsed at his intoxicating scent and firm body, which was rigid in all the right places. We slipped into the backseat of the cab, the mood between us giddy. We were really doing it—going out on a proper date. The tone of our relationship felt totally different. Braydon's wide smile and roaming hands had me giggling as we rode to the restaurant.

After he paid the driver, he helped me from the car and led me inside a dimly lit Italian restaurant with exposed brick walls, flickering candles, and the scent of garlic in the air. My stomach grumbled loudly as the hostess seated us at the booth in the front, overlooking the bustling sidewalk and busy street. The fading sunlight warmed the mahogany table and cast everything in a pretty, romantic glow. I liked being out with Braydon. I couldn't help but notice people casting glances our direction. We looked cute together. He smartly dressed in a button-down navy shirt and gray slacks; me in my slim-fit black ankle pants, flats, and a red sweater with chunky gold jewelry.

We flipped open the menus and decided on a bottle of wine and an appetizer just as our server appeared. Once the wine arrived, he lifted his glass of Shiraz to mine.

"Cheers."

"To?" I inquired.

His lazy smile lifted as he thought it over. "To being out."

Out. I pondered the meaning while I swirled the ruby-colored liquid in the glass. Out in public? Or out, as in, out of the closet as a couple? I'd give myself a headache trying to solve that question, so instead I just lifted the glass to my lips. The spicy, peppery flavors of black currant and tannins hit my palate and instantly relaxed me. I took several gulps of the wine to calm my nerves. I briefly wondered if he was still worried about his ex—I knew that being out with a woman was a big deal for him. It made me sit up just a little taller in my seat.

Having not seen him on a regular basis like I'd grown used to, I wondered what Braydon had been up to. "Have you been working much?" I asked, accepting a refill of my wine.

"Quite a bit, actually. I just filmed a commercial for a

sports car last week, and I've booked several print jobs recently. And in my free time I've been helping Ben on the finances for the charity."

"I didn't know you knew about finance."

He nodded. "It was my major in college. And I figure if I can help them out, then they don't have to pay someone to do it and can use their funds for good instead of operating expenses."

I smiled at his thoughtfulness. The more I thought about it, the more impressed I was with his unending loyalty to Ben and Emmy. He was really one of the most dedicated friends I'd ever met. I didn't appreciate that side of him enough.

We coordinated our orders to include two very different dishes so we could share them. As we ate pesto ravioli and spicy shrimp with linguine, Braydon asked about my work. I chattered on and he listened attentively. I described the tedious nature of my job and the projects I was currently running. I figured he'd be bored to tears within minutes, but Braydon always surprised me. He asked thoughtful questions and probed deeper a few times, too. It was nice to have an adult conversation that was more than just flirty banter.

Something else was stewing in the back of my mind. He'd told me about his failed past relationship and invited me out to a nice dinner . . . so I should probably feel grateful and not pry, but something told me there was more to the story. Following my gut instinct, I pushed him a little harder.

"I can't help feeling like something else happened in your past to turn you against relationships so completely. I want

you to know, you can open up to me. You can trust me, Bray."
He smiled, but didn't say anything else. I pressed on. "If the
right girl came along, do you think you'd be open for something more?"

He pondered my question, looking down at his plate.
Then his blue eyes slid up to mine. "She'd have to be one hell
of a girl." He smiled, his dimple taunting me.

"Why are you like this?" I held up a hand. "And don't
say it's just because of your past. I hate to think one girl had
this power over you. Something else must have happened."
Something prevented me from mentioning Katrina. I knew
he'd had at least one successful relationship, but I doubted
he'd take too kindly to me digging into his past.

Braydon released a heavy exhale and set down his fork.
It wasn't a conversation he wanted to have, but I could tell he
was willing to try. For me. "Let's just say I was with someone
who fucked with my head. It's made me wary of starting anything serious again."

I waited, watching him and silently turning the bracelet
on my wrist. I sensed there was something more he wanted
to say.

"My mom . . ." He coughed and cleared his throat before starting again. "She developed early-onset dementia.
She got so bad, so unstable and untrusting of everyone, she
had to be moved into a permanent-care facility. My dad lost
himself when that happened. I watched how losing my mom
utterly changed my dad. He went from this vibrant, strong
man, looking forward to retirement and traveling, to a shell

of his former self. He had to go on antianxiety medication, and when he wasn't at Mom's side, he just sat in front of the TV and zoned out. Retirement was put on hold to pay for her extremely pricey care. That all happened at the same time that I found out the girl I'd grown close to was batshit crazy."

I reached out and held his hand. "I'm sorry. Is your mom…" *Better,* I prayed.

"She passed away last year."

"I'm so sorry."

He nodded at my acknowledgment. There was nothing more to say. Braydon wasn't some shallow player, as I'd feared. There were deeper reasons that explained how he had become this person, external forces that had shaped his outlook and willingness to give himself over and fall in love. My heart hurt for him. I knew I needed to be patient and let him heal and find his own way. I just hoped that I was at the end of that path.

After that heavy conversation, we ate in silence until we were both full. We refused dessert, even though the cheesecake and the tiramisu were calling my name. I knew I better not overdo it.

"Thank you for tonight," I murmured after Braydon had settled the check with our server.

He lifted my hand to his lips and planted a soft kiss on my palm. "You're welcome, dear."

It all felt so normal and datelike, yet it was such a new

experience being out with him like this. I liked it. A lot. And I especially loved how he'd opened up to me a little more. I couldn't believe he'd shared all that about his mom and dad's relationship. I could see why that would make him wary about love. But it only made me want to love him more. He needed it—deserved it—and I wanted to be the one to care for him.

After dinner, we stood on the sidewalk as the traffic and pedestrians buzzed past us. I was full and happy and slightly tipsy from the wine. I was trying to keep my expectations in check, but I wanted nothing more than for him to whisk me back to his place and show me where he lived. Take me to his bed. I hoped his pillows smelled like him. I wondered if he'd be messy or neat. A minimalist or a hoarder. Would his kitchen be barren and seldom used, or would it bear the evidence that he enjoyed cooking at home? I'd gotten another peek inside the heart of Braydon, but there were so many other little things I was curious about.

"Are we going back to your place?" I whispered, nuzzling against the warmth of his neck. I loved the way his stubble lightly grazed my skin.

"Not tonight."

I paused. "Oh."

"Can I take you home?"

I thought it over. I didn't want to ruin the evening. *Tonight was progress*, I had to keep reminding myself as we waited for a passing cab to stop.

"I could come over for a little while," he offered.

"I don't think that's a good idea."

"I thought this was what you wanted?" Confusion etched into his brow.

I shook my head. Going out was just half of the equation. I wouldn't give in this easily. "No apartment, no sex."

"Why is that so important to you?"

"It just is. I don't want to fall into the same pattern with you. Where you live is a huge fucking deal. Someone's place says a lot about them. I don't want to take the next step if you're going to keep holding back."

"Can't I have just one secret?"

"Yes. Harmless secrets, like whether or not you pee in the shower—or if you've ever farted on the subway and blamed it on someone else."

He broke out in laughter, despite the heavy moment. "You're too much. You know that?"

I narrowed my eyes at him.

"And for the record, I don't pee in the shower."

"Yeah right," I scoffed. "I thought all guys did that. It's like a locker room thing—crossing streams and playing swords . . ."

He shook his head. "Nope. Not this guy. I use the toilet. While the shower water heats up."

I chuckled. "Me too." My foolish brain cataloged that it was just another of the many things we had in common. "Still, this is a big deal to me, Braydon. Huge, in fact. I want us to trust each other. If you can't even give me your address, then maybe we need more time."

He nodded. "You're right. Goodnight then."

"Night," I said a bit more harshly than I meant to. I turned from him and slipped into the cab that had stopped at the curb, feeling mixed emotions about the way our first date had ended.

17

Braydon and I continued seeing each other casually—just as friends. *Yay, me.* We'd met up for coffee, drinks with Ben and Emmy, a couple of movies, and lunch on our own. It was unclear if our outings were just as friends or something more. We hadn't been to my apartment again, and we hadn't so much as kissed. It appeared we were at a standstill. I needed something beyond the physical, and he'd said he'd missed our friendship, so this seemed to be our new arrangement for now.

Emmy was more confused than ever about things. For all intents and purposes we appeared to be dating, yet we both insisted to Ben and Emmy, separately, that things were platonic.

"Let me get this straight," she said, setting down her empty champagne glass on the tray of a passing waiter. "First, you weren't dating but you were sleeping together . . . and now you're dating but nothing's happening between you two?"

"Exactly." I grabbed a cheese puff from the tray of a cute waiter as he whizzed past.

"I don't get you guys."

"Welcome to the club," I muttered, popping the morsel into my mouth. I hadn't mentioned to Emmy the things I'd learned about Braydon—about his past relationship or his mother's passing. They felt too private, and I wanted to protect him.

We were in Los Angeles for a fashion event, and Emmy and I were currently mingling at an afterparty, waiting for the guys to arrive. So far, I hadn't seen much of Braydon— we were staying in separate hotel rooms, and he'd been busy with the fashion show, photo shoots, and appearances. It was all for the launch of a new California lifestyle and surf brand. Braydon, with his messy hair and piercing blue eyes, was the perfect spokesmodel, and he was garnering a lot of positive buzz. For the past two days, Emmy and I had spent our time at the Santa Monica pier, lying on the beach during the days when the guys were working, then joining them in the evenings for dinner. Tonight was our last night there, and I hoped to sneak in at least a little private time with the man of the hour.

"Let's go see what hors d'oeuvres they have over there." I pointed to the far end of the room where another banquet table was set with goodies. Emmy chuckled and nodded, following me across the room.

Just as I was biting into the biggest chocolate-covered strawberry I'd ever seen, Ben and Braydon appeared. His eyes zeroed in on my mouth as the berry was suspended precariously between my teeth. A little chill zipped up my spine. He was still watching me, or more specifically, my mouth. His eyes were trained on what I was doing to the strawberry. I felt the chocolate begin to melt at the contact of my tongue. I licked the melted droplet of warm chocolate from my bottom lip, toying with Braydon. I saw him wince. My teeth lightly grazed the flesh of the berry, just like Braydon used to do to me. He'd lightly bite my neck, my collarbone, my nipples. I shivered at the memory. Sinking my teeth fully into the berry, bursts of sweet juice combined with the flavor of the bitter dark chocolate and caused a low moan to emanate in the back of my throat.

Braydon stalked over in two long strides, completely closing the distance between us, his pulse jumping at the base of his neck. I'd never seen him look so serious, but his gaze was locked on mine as if I'd done something terribly wrong. One hand curled around my hip and the other removed the stem of the berry from my fingers. "Careful there, kitten, or that dessert isn't the only thing that'll be in your mouth."

My breathing faltered. I worried my damn heart was going to give out. The way he was looking at me was pure sex. Like he owned me. My brain screamed for air, yet I remained rooted there, breathless and completely at his mercy.

"Breathe for me," he whispered, dropping the stem into a nearby wastebasket.

I sucked in a breath of much-needed oxygen. *There, much better.*

Braydon's deep blue gaze remained trained on mine, watching me, reading every emotion that flitted across my brain. I wanted him. And he knew it.

Several tense heartbeats later, Braydon was whisked away by an older man in a suit and I was left with an ache the size of the Grand Canyon between my thighs.

Damn him for still being able to get to me like that. I was supposed to be taunting *him*. Not the other way around. But he'd turned the table on me. My seductive berry-eating trick was being used against me as my head filled with thoughts of me on my knees, taking his hot length into my mouth, flicking my tongue along his steely shaft until I found the barbell piercing his head.

Mmm ... memories ...

Braydon was still chatting quietly with the older man, but they'd now been joined by two beautiful blond bombshells in barely there cocktail dresses. Game over. No way I could compete with them. He remained with the group, but his eyes strayed to mine every so often to let me know he was still thinking of me, of our little encounter just moments ago. The blonde to his left leaned in close to him, brushing her breasts against his chest as she whispered something meant only for his ears. Braydon pulled back ever so slightly and shook his head, no doubt refusing whatever it was she was offering.

My heart soared.

His sexy blue eyes found mine once again. I felt a bolt of heat radiate from my belly down to my core. He was becoming harder and harder to resist. But until he fully let me in, I knew I needed to stand my ground.

Teasing him just a little more, though, was something I couldn't resist.

In the elevator ride back to our rooms, Ben and Emmy were in their own private bliss, holding hands, whispering to each other and laughing at their own inside jokes—which left Braydon and me standing in stony silence, awkwardness hanging in the air around us. Leaning forward to punch the button to my floor, my bottom accidently brushed the front of Braydon's slacks. His entire body stiffened and he let out a muted curse. My lips curled up in a smile. It seemed as though I ruffled his feathers every bit as much as he ruffled mine. Good to know. I stood a little taller in my heels, feeling proud. When I turned back to look in his direction, Braydon's expression caught me off guard. Intensity radiated from him. Something was off with him. But I had no clue what.

"Would you mind walking me to my room?" I asked, my tone low.

He gave a stiff nod. "Of course I will."

Ben and Emmy exited the elevator on their floor and Braydon remained by my side, riding up several more floors and following me to my hotel room once the lift stopped. I fumbled a bit with the key card thanks to my shaking hands. I had no game plan, no clue what I was doing. All I knew was that I wasn't ready for the night to be over. I wasn't ready to say good-bye to Braydon.

Once we made it inside the room, I flipped on a table-side lamp and Braydon turned to me. "Are you okay?"

"Fine," I breathed.

Two fingers lifted my chin and his eyes searched mine. Slowly, achingly slowly, he lowered his mouth to mine. "Don't lie to me," he exhaled against my lips.

I shook my head. "Never."

The anticipation of his mouth so close that I could feel the warmth of his breath put my entire body on hyperalert. I wanted him to kiss me more than I wanted my next breath. It'd been too long. Too many lonely nights remembering all the ways he used to pleasure my body. His mouth closed over mine in a kiss that started off sweet and innocent but quickly turned into something hungry and hot. He nibbled at my bottom lip until my lips parted, then his tongue sought entrance and began rubbing against mine. Holy hell, he knew how to kiss. I suckled at his tongue and he groaned into my mouth. Those sounds were like pouring gasoline on the flames inside me. Everything ignited at once. I needed him. Wanted him. Consequences be damned. I fought with his shirt, grabbing fistfuls of it and yanking. He'd already succeeded in ruining me. I might as well go for the gusto. Braydon caught on and broke the kiss only long enough to tear his shirt off. My hands found his belt and I began tugging.

"Slow down, kitten." His big hands captured my jaw and he whispered against my lips. "There's no rush."

He was wrong, though. There was a rush. If I was going to go through with this, it was best to get caught up in the heat of passion—to not let myself slow down to think this through. I dropped to my knees and pulled down his zipper while looking up to meet his gaze.

Braydon's teeth sunk into his bottom lip as he watched me with wide eyes.

As I tugged down his boxer briefs and dress slacks in one motion, his thick cock sprang free to greet me. Good God, it'd been too long. I'd missed this thing. How that was even possible, I had no clue, only that it was an absolute fact. I missed the breathing sounds he made when I pleased him, missed the way his abdominals tightened when he was getting close, and yes, I missed his naughty piercing. A lot.

Gripping the base of him with one hand, I guided him into the warmth of my mouth. He let out a string of curse words and fisted a hand in my hair. Pushing past the initial gag reflex, I took him as deep as I could and felt his knees lock.

"Fucking hell, kitten." His thumb smoothed up and down my cheek as he looked down at me with wonder. "Don't make me fall for you . . ."

He couldn't be sweet right now. My poor tattered and broken heart couldn't take it. This was supposed to be a hookup. Nothing more. I gripped him harder and stroked as I paid extra attention to his piercing, suckling his head into my mouth and rubbing my tongue along the barbell.

He let out a ragged groan.

Gripping my arms, seconds later Braydon hauled me to my feet and stripped off my dress and heels in a matter of moments. I stood before him in a pair of black panties and nothing more, and even those were tugged down my legs before I could blink. He was every bit as intent on getting me naked as I had been with him. My heart raced.

Lifting me over his shoulder, Braydon carted me to the nearby bed and deposited me unceremoniously in the center, then began crawling up my body, spreading my legs wide with his hands. Kissing a wet path up my body, he moved with calculated precision. For all the rushing we were both doing, things suddenly slowed. He was making this about me, being too sweet, too considerate. I couldn't take it.

"Inside me . . ." I gripped his shoulders and tugged him farther up the bed. "I need you inside me." No sense pretending this was some romantic lovemaking session.

His eyes met mine and a low growl tore from his throat. No more words needed to be exchanged. Braydon's hand captured his length and he aligned himself with my entrance before slowly pushing forward. He remembered that I needed time to adjust to his size and acted accordingly, letting me get accustomed while his jaw tensed with need.

Don't make me fall for you . . .

His words rang in my head with each thrust. He entered me and slowly pulled out, rocking against me in the most deliciously exquisite rhythm. I gripped his firm ass, pressing him closer, needing him to fully claim me, and whimpered when he hit just the right spot.

"Kitten," he whispered sweetly in my ear. "You feel so fucking good."

Gentle bites and sucking kisses at my neck brought back a rush of memories. Too many good memories to count. Tears formed in my eyes and I squeezed them tight to prevent any from leaking out. I couldn't let him see me break down. I just needed to stay in the moment, to feel every bit of pleasure he was giving me. And I wanted to please him; he'd been through so much pain . . . maybe we could heal each other.

Braydon brought my knees together, closing my legs and kneeled in front of me, slowly pulling out and pushing in until he was fully sated. Feeling him like this was beautiful torture . . . he was deeper than ever before.

Arching my back, I lost myself in the rhythm, in the sensations his body elicited from mine. All too soon, I was moaning his name as I came apart. He followed me over the edge, burying his hands in my hair and exhaling a soft curse as he came.

18

Once we were back home, it was as if nothing had changed. We should have been nominated for Oscars for the amazing job we did acting like nothing had happened between us in LA. Braydon texted occasionally, asking me for coffee or for a walk in the park. Even though it was painful to see him, to be near him, I usually caved in and said yes. But we were still strictly friends and hadn't slipped up with any physical contact again. It seemed we were more careful around each other than ever before—going out of our way to avoid touching at all costs. When he reached for the bill, I conveniently needed something from my purse, and when I grabbed a sugar packet for my coffee, his hands tucked themselves into his pockets.

I was still waiting for him to realize that he couldn't live without me, just like Emmy kept saying he would. So far, it was a no-go. And I was more depressed than ever.

It hadn't helped that I'd come down with the world's worst case of the flu. For the past several days, I felt achy and exhausted and had been regularly puking my guts out. The first few days I'd called in sick to work, but now it seemed that my body was growing accustomed to living with the sickness, so I ventured into work but kept a plastic garbage bag under my desk for when the urge struck. Oh, joy.

A text from Braydon was a nice distraction later that afternoon.

Braydon: Hey you up for grabbing coffee or a drink tonight?

I stared down at my phone. Another half-hearted attempt. I didn't want a coffee date out with a friend at this point. I wanted him, no holds barred. Even if I had wanted to say yes, the crappy way I felt prevented me. I hadn't kept down coffee in nearly a week. I'd taken to drinking ginger ale in the morning. And though the relaxing buzz that came from a nice glass of wine sounded nice, I doubted I could stomach that either.

Me: No thanks, I'll have to take a rain check. I have the flu.

Braydon: Shit. That sucks. Let me know if you need anything—I'm on it.

Me: Thanks, I will.

And that was that.

Until two days later.

I was home. Saturday, thank god.

Braydon: Hey, you feeling better?

I didn't want him to worry, to insist on coming over with soup or something, and I wouldn't put that past him. The truth was I just wanted to be alone. I felt like shit. I looked worse. I was in sweatpants with greasy, matted hair and I

wanted to stay that way, warm under my covers for the rest
of the day.

Me: *I'm on the mend, but not there yet. Sorry to disappoint.*

Braydon: *You never disappoint. I just wish you were feeling*
better.

I released a heavy sigh. He was in his famous sweet, gentle-
manly mode. He held my beating heart in the palm of his hand,
little did he know. He had the ability to crush it or put me back
together, make me whole. I feared what he'd choose. I knew
he'd been through hell in his past relationships, losing his mom
and watching what his dad went through afterward.

I needed to swallow my pride and move on. Maybe he'd
never be ready—or maybe I wasn't the girl to get him there.
Something inside me told me I was, though. I was the girl for
the job. He'd said himself that the chemistry we shared wasn't
something he'd ever experienced. Me neither. That had to
count for something, right?

Every remembered whisper, every sweet thing he'd done,
the way he'd owned my body, made me crave him. I shuddered, and not from the fever chills wracking my body.

Braydon: *Can I do anything? I don't like this.*

He didn't like it? Shit, I was the one who'd lost five pounds
in the last week alone. Actually, I counted that as the one and
only benefit of this flu.

Me: *Nothing you can do, but thanks. I think it just needs to*
run its course.

Braydon: *Well I'm checking on you tomorrow, no matter what.*

I appreciated his concern, I truly did, but it wasn't making it any easier on my heart. The one organ that hadn't been affected by the flu from hell. What I'd done to deserve this, I had no clue.

I went to bed that night with my head swimming from the combo of nighttime sleep meds and pain reliever and collapsed into a heavy sleep.

When Braydon texted in the morning, the threat of him coming over and actually discovering my raggedy state prompted me to lie.

Braydon: Hey kitten, feeling better yet?

Me: Yes, actually, quite a lot.

Braydon: That's awesome. I need you to meet me somewhere today. It's important.

An address off Fifth Street followed in a separate text. He wanted me to venture all the way to the West Village near NYU.

Keeping up my ruse of being healthy, I agreed. I had no idea how I'd ride the subway, which was likely to feel like a bad roller coaster to my ravaged stomach. Big-girl panties today. Suck it up, buttercup.

Just the act of getting showered and ready was exhausting, but I rallied. Leaving my apartment forty minutes later, I was presentable in dark-washed jeans, a bright pink cotton knit sweater, and my tennis shoes. *Here goes nothing.* I didn't know where I was meeting him, but I figured casual dress would be fine. Braydon was never one for fancy outings.

Once I arrived in the neighborhood, I didn't know what I was looking for since he'd given me an address and not the name of the establishment we were meeting at. It was a rather artsy area. I passed by Tompkins Square Park, where street performers sang and danced for tips, and a poetry club that was open to walk-ins. I approached a building bearing the address he'd given me. A rehabbed industrial building in soft gray brick with a big red front door.

I texted him, unsure of what to do next.

Me: I'm here. What is this place?

Braydon: My apartment. Come inside. Sixth floor. Apartment 601.

What? Whoa. I suddenly felt dizzy with the cars and people zooming past. He'd invited me over? Simple as that?

I headed inside and took the elevator up to the sixth floor. I arrived at unit 601 and gave a light knock on the door. The door swung open to reveal a smiling Braydon. He pulled me to his chest and gave me a squeeze. "Hi," he murmured against my hair.

"Hello," I returned, still a bit dazed.

When he released me, my eyes darted behind him to take in the light-filled loft. It had tall ceilings that were crisscrossed with wooden beams, an exposed brick wall running along the living space, and floor-to-ceiling windows looking out onto the city street below. It was charming and cozy. Just like him. Simple furniture and a color scheme with dark gray, tan, and splashes of blue made it feel inviting.

"Come in." He ushered me inside and shut the door. The scent that enveloped me was every bit Braydon. All male and warm and delicious. I wanted to just stand here and inhale, but Braydon's hand on my lower back guided me into the living room.

"Would you like a tour?"

I nodded slowly. His eyes locked on mine and told me he knew that this was a big step in the right direction, which made me happy, though I wasn't totally sure what to make of this gesture. Was he opening his life up for me?

I followed him forward, stepping onto a comfortable shaggy rug that warmed up the space. The wooden plank floors creaked lightly as we walked. I liked that I had somewhere to picture Braydon when we were apart.

He showed me the living room, which included a framed photograph of his mom and dad, his tiny but ultraneat kitchen that contained an impressive coffee and espresso maker that I was dying to try. I imagined waking up to the smell of roasting beans. Then we ventured down a narrow hallway that led to his bathroom, with a glass-enclosed shower, and his bedroom at the far end. It was open and bright with a large bed dressed in white and gray linens. He had a tall dresser and a small writing desk and a chair positioned against the far wall. It was here that I imagined him working on the finances for Ben and Emmy's charity. Black-and-white photography prints were hung on the walls and a small throw rug was positioned at the foot of his bed. It was a lovely room, but I was hit with a pang of sadness that he was only just now sharing it.

"Kitten?"

My gaze lifted to him, pushing away the solemn thoughts. "It's a beautiful place."

His frown lines deepened. "You don't look well." His hand raised to smooth down an unruly lock of hair. "You're pale. Are you sure you feel okay?"

"I'm fine," I lied. My stomach was turning somersaults, but that feeling was nothing compared to the uncertainty and sadness in my heart. "Maybe we could just go sit down."

He nodded. "Of course."

We returned to the living room and I slumped onto the sofa. The throw pillows smelled like him, and even though I'd wanted nothing more than to be here at his place, it now felt too intimate, too personal and I was too weak to handle all the emotions it caused.

Braydon leaned over me and placed a palm against my cheek. "Hmm, you feel okay. Warm, but not overly so."

I blinked up at him. The journey across the city and the emotional backlash of finally being here had caught up with me. I needed a nap. I yawned.

"I'm going to make you some homemade chicken noodle soup. That sound good?"

I nodded, weakly. "Yes, thank you."

I dozed while he cooked and woke a short time later to the sounds of him moving about in the kitchen. I sat up, stretched, and ventured in to join him. The discarded remains of chopped carrots, celery, and onions sat on a nearby cutting board and a pot of soup was bubbling on the stove. Braydon glanced up from where he was stirring the concoction.

"It's almost ready. Just waiting for the noodles to become tender."

"Okay."

"Go sit. I'll serve you."

"Do you have crackers?" I asked.

"Sure do. I'll bring them."

I smiled and went back to the couch to wait. A few minutes later, Braydon emerged carrying a bowl of steaming hot soup and a box of crackers.

"Here, eat up. This was my mom's recipe and she made it for me whenever I was sick."

"Thank you." I started in on a cracker first, needing to test my stomach. It went down easily enough, so I moved on to the soup while Braydon supervised. "It's delicious." I could taste a hint of parsley and the warm broth was divine. I ate the entire bowlful.

"More?" he asked.

I shook my head. My belly was full for the first time in weeks. No need to tempt fate. I lay back and rested my head on the sofa.

Braydon played with my hair and hummed quietly while I tried to relax.

Opening my eyes several minutes later, I turned to face him. "Well, the soup was delicious, but I should probably get out of your way. I'm not going to be very good company to-night."

"Stop it. You're not going anywhere. I invited you here because I wanted to spend time with you."

I narrowed my eyes. "Why did you invite me over?" *Today. Finally.*

"Because it was time. And you belong here with me." His hand closed around mine and he gave it a squeeze. My heart pumped wildly in my chest. "And I didn't invite you over for any funny business. I know I lost those privileges a while ago."

I looked down at our intertwined hands, thankful that he didn't mention our slip-up in LA a few weeks ago. "So what do you propose we do then?" If I was feeling better, there would have probably been a hint of suggestiveness in my tone, but I truly felt too crummy.

"We stay in tonight, and not because we're hiding out here, but so you can take it easy and heal. We'll watch a movie and get some more of that magic soup inside of you."

I wanted to make a quip about the soup being the only thing tonight that was getting inside me, but I was too weak and exhausted to even be funny. Sad day right there. "Okay," I agreed. Honestly, a movie and cuddling with Bray sounded like the perfect evening. Much better than sulking alone in my apartment for the millionth time.

Braydon pulled a woolly throw blanket from the back of the sofa and covered us both. "Come here, kitten. Lean on me."

I did as I was told. God, he felt perfect. This felt perfect.

How did he not feel this between us? He lay down on the couch and pulled me closer, aligning our bodies until we were pressed nice and close. As great as this moment was, there was still a conversation we needed to have. I needed some answers about this puzzle of a man. I looked up and met his eyes, bringing my palm to his cheek. "Thank you for bringing me here today."

"You're welcome." He closed his eyes, relaxing while my fingertips grazed lightly across his stubble.

"Bray?"

"Hmm . . ."

"I have a few things I need to say."

His eyes slowly opened.

I took a deep, fortifying breath to steady myself. "I know there are things in your past that are preventing you from moving forward. And I'm so glad you told me about your mom. It helps me understand things a lot better. But as for your ex, I just wanted to say whatever she did to you, I'm sorry. We can take things slow, do things your way."

He remained silently watching me and blinked twice. "Fuck." That single word was his acknowledgment that I was right, and that I knew more than he realized. "What are you saying, exactly?"

"That I accept you. And your past, and these flaws that make it impossible for you to have a relationship."

"You don't understand what you're saying."

"Then tell me. Explain it to me," I begged. I was here, in

his apartment, and as far as I was concerned, there was no better place or time to have this discussion.

"I already told you there was a girl."

"And? You're no longer capable of relationships?"

He frowned. "Not exactly, no."

I waited, holding my breath, hoping and praying he'd open up and explain it all to me finally.

He licked his lips. "It's just that my last relationship ended disastrously."

I listened silently as he opened himself up to me. We lay side by side on the sofa and Braydon told me a little more about the story he'd begun earlier—that his last girlfriend became unstable once he broke things off, and she began harassing him and his family. She couldn't accept that things were over. That he couldn't date in the public eye, because she'd harass the new girls he began seeing after her. I could only imagine how the stress of that, coupled with the loss of his mother, made him hesitant to enter into another serious relationship.

"What finally happened, with the girl?" I pressed him. We hadn't covered that last time.

He shrugged. "She's still not over me. I told you I have a restraining order against her. She sends long handwritten letters to my agency since she doesn't know my address anymore. And she somehow showed up at a photo shoot of mine a few months ago and I had security remove her."

Oh my god. That was where I'd met Katrina.

"She's a stalker, basically."

"What's her name?" I asked, my voice shaking.

"Kat."

Holy mother. "I-I know her. I mean, I-I met her . . ."

His brows pinched together. "Where? How?"

"At that photo shoot. The day I came, I met a girl there—she said she was a fan of your work, but later she admitted that you two dated. She said her name was Katrina."

"Shit," he cursed and rose to his feet and began pacing in front of the sofa. "You spoke to her?"

I nodded. "Yes."

"You didn't tell her anything about yourself or me—did you?"

I swallowed a hard lump in my throat. "Well, um, sort of, but I had no idea that . . ."

"Fuck!" he swore loudly and pushed his hands into his hair. "Ellie, this is important. Tell me what you told her."

"We met for a drink. We've texted . . . but it was all innocent, I swear."

"How could you do that, Ellie?"

He continued pacing. "You know how private I am. Didn't you think that maybe, just maybe, I had good reason for being so guarded?"

I rose to my feet, standing directly in front of him. This wasn't my fault. And I truly believed I hadn't done anything wrong. "It's not like I told her much—I didn't even know where you lived until today. It was harmless girl talk, commiserating together over broken hearts. Not that I would ex-

All or Nothing   231

pect you to understand that—your heart's never been in this game."

The pulse in his neck was racing, and his eyes were blazing with anger, but Braydon remained silent.

"You know what. Never mind. It was stupid to think coming here meant something." I grabbed my purse and stuffed my feet into my shoes. "Good-bye Braydon." I was out the door and in the elevator without a backward glance.

19

A few days later, I couldn't ignore Braydon's constant phone calls and texts any longer. I agreed to meet him for coffee at a central location.

When I arrived, Braydon was already seated at a table by the front window with a mug in front of him and another that was for me, I presumed. Coffee had been too rough on my postflu stomach and I'd been avoiding it for several weeks now.

I approached the table and Braydon rose to his feet. He looked tired. Still handsome as always, but dark circles ringed his eyes and the usual mischief sparkling in them was missing. "Thank you for meeting me."

I nodded. He wasn't getting jack squat out of me. I was here. That was all.

"I wanted to apologize, and explain everything to you."

"I'm listening."

He nodded, and fiddled with his coffee mug. "First and

foremost, I'm sorry how I behaved. I overreacted. You did nothing wrong, and I see that now. I just . . . get a little tense thinking that Katrina is still, after all this time, trying to infiltrate my life, and used you to gain information."

I listened while he spoke, but something wasn't sitting right with me. I thought of the girl I'd met and the sadness I'd seen in her eyes. "Did you ever consider that maybe she just needs closure from you?"

He blinked at me several times. "What do you mean?"

God, men . . . they could be so dense. "Like to hear from you why it ended, what went wrong, so she can accept it and move on from that time in her life . . ."

He shook his head. "It's not that simple."

"I think it might be." I was probably taking a gamble, but something told me a little closure coming from Braydon himself could be exactly the thing to solve this. Only I had no idea if he'd be open to that. "Would you be willing to talk with her?"

"Break my restraining order by voluntarily meeting with her?"

I nodded.

"Shit, Ellie. If you think it will work, why the hell not. But you're going to be there for the conversation. I can't be alone with her."

"Of course I am." Something told me I'd likely be moderating the conversation between them. "Shall I text her? See if she's free?"

He raised his eyebrows. "Why the hell not?" He smirked.

I dug out my phone and sent the text through. I debated whether or not to tell her she'd be facing Braydon, and in the end, decided to be honest, hoping she'd still agree to come.

Me: Hey, are you free to meet now for coffee? I'm with Braydon. It's important.

Kat: Okay . . . I'll come.

"She's on her way."

"Lovely," Braydon murmured.

I could tell he wasn't too thrilled with the idea of facing his crazy ex-girlfriend right now, but I believed this could solve things once and for all between Braydon and his past. Which was really all I ever wanted.

Soon Kat arrived, and the gleeful expression on her face when she spotted Braydon was slightly disconcerting.

"Hey, Kat," I greeted her with a one-armed hug and Braydon's eyes widened. I didn't think he was expecting that we were quite so close.

"Um, hi. Hi, Braydon."

"Hello," he returned coolly.

"Would you like to grab some coffee?" Might as well be a good hostess since I'd arranged this awkward encounter.

"I'm fine." She sat down, joining us at the table so that she was seated directly across from me and Braydon.

Somehow I found the right words to explain to them both, carefully, that a last meeting seemed to be in order and my goal was to help them move past the tension that still existed between them. Katrina looked hopeful . . . while Braydon looked slightly annoyed.

Once I'd given my little speech, Katrina folded her hands on the table and stared up at Bray. "How have you been? I've been trying to reach you."

Braydon's eyes locked with mine as if to say *I told you so* and he released a heavy sigh. "This has to stop, Kat. Why are you still doing this? Trying to contact me through my agency and now getting close to Ellie. It's been two years."

Katrina swallowed and looked down, her poise faltering. "All I've ever wanted was to understand why."

"Why what?" Braydon asked.

"Why things ended between us. I thought you loved me, but you started to become distant over time, going away on jobs and forgetting to call me when you landed, and eventually you just . . ." She stopped herself and took a deep, fortifying breath. "I want to know why I lost you."

Wow. Okay, now we were getting somewhere.

"Fuck." Braydon rubbed his hands across his face. "Because I was twenty-three years old at the time. Because I was immature. An asshole. Not at all ready to commit to one girl. And you wanted things from me I couldn't give you."

Katrina continued to watch him and listen in silent fascination.

"And there reached a point where I knew you were more serious about the relationship than I was. Once I broke things off, quite honestly your behavior worried me. Calling my parents' house, questioning my dad about where I was. Breaking into my old apartment and staying there while I was traveling."

A cold chill zipped down my spine. I hadn't realized how far Katrina's odd behavior went.

Braydon continued, "It wasn't healthy. I thought cutting things off with you cold turkey and not stringing you along was for the best. But when you didn't relent after a few months, my manager at the agency suggested the restraining order. He said he'd seen these types of things escalate before."

"Oh." Katrina looked down at her hands. "I loved you. I just needed to understand what I'd done wrong. I needed closure. And to know you were okay."

My heart broke for her.

"You didn't do anything wrong when we were together," Braydon's tone softened. "I liked you a lot. I wouldn't have dated you for eight months if I didn't."

"It was nine months," Katrina interjected.

I watched the back-and-forth between them like a game of Ping-Pong. An extremely awkward and tense game of Ping-Pong.

"Right. Nine months. But, you were ready for more, and I didn't want to be tied down. We were at an impasse. So I figured it was best to move on."

"I see," she said, her voice growing shaky. She looked like she might break down in tears, so I carefully placed a hand on her shoulder.

"Are you okay?"

She blinked back tears and nodded. "Yes. This helps. A lot, actually."

I looked at Braydon. *See, dumbass.*

"I spent the last two years wondering what I did wrong and wishing I knew what I could have changed," Katrina said, braving a glance at Braydon once again.

"Don't change. I hate to be cliché and say it wasn't you, it was me. But it's true. You will find a man who loves you and wants all the things you do. I just wasn't him."

She smiled weakly and nodded. "Wow, you sound like my mother. And you're both right. It's time to move on and open myself up to new possibilities."

I wrapped an arm around Katrina and gave her a hug. "Good luck."

"You guys, too."

Katrina left a few moments later, and I could see in her eyes that she needed to be alone, probably have herself a good cry. I hoped this experience had been cathartic for her. I could already feel the growth they'd both experienced, even if it hadn't all sunk in yet.

The mood between me and Braydon was somber as we left the coffee shop. Something between us had shifted and I wasn't entirely sure what. I'd seen his past and been part of helping him work through some skeletons in his closet. I should have felt lighter, freer, but instead I just felt sad. Sad for Katrina that she'd wasted two years, sad for Braydon that he'd lived as a recluse after his last relationship went so wrong.

I wondered why it took two years for them to have this conversation. But maybe the time was necessary. It provided time for emotions to cool and them both to be a little wiser and more mature to face the consequences of their actions. I was happy to help them solve it. It just still felt so senseless.

"Thank you for that," he said.

"You're welcome." I was just glad it went so well.

"I'm sorry my baggage got in the way of us. I feel like an ass."

"Guys are asses sometimes. You were young."

Those pretty baby blues of his latched on to mine. "It's no excuse."

I nodded. It was refreshing to hear him take responsibility for his actions. And actually I agreed. He should have had that conversation with her a long time ago. That restraining order may have never been needed. Katrina could have moved on with her life much sooner, and Braydon would never have instituted his rules for relationship-free arrangements. And I might have had an actual shot at dating the one guy I'd fallen for. It all just felt pointless. Then again, maybe the Katrina of two years ago wouldn't have listened and would have fought hard to win him back no matter what he'd said.

I sensed that the three of us would all be moving on bettered from our conversation today—only I didn't know which direction Braydon and I would be going.

"You want to go home, and order in?" he asked as we stood facing each other on the sidewalk.

"No thanks. I'm tired and a bubble bath sounds nice." I just needed some alone time to sort through my feelings, and

I thought it might do Braydon some good to do the same. Today had been a lot to take in.

He nodded in understanding. Truthfully, the heaviness of the past hour had affected us both. I could tell he wouldn't mind being alone with his thoughts for the night.

"I'll see ya." I gave him one last hug and left.

I made it only a few steps, though, before the coffee was coming back up into a nearby trash can. *Lovely.* After I'd gotten sick, I wiped my mouth on my sleeve and ventured a glance over my shoulder. Braydon had seen the entire thing. *Shit.*

He was at my side, supporting me with an arm around my waist in a matter of seconds. "What's wrong? Are you still sick?"

I let out a groan and closed my eyes. "I'm sorry. I think it was the coffee. It was too much for my stomach."

"Don't be sorry, I'm just worried about you."

I leaned into his side, thankful for the support. I just wanted to lie down in my bed, safe and warm.

"How long have you been sick? Be honest with me."

"A month," I croaked.

"Fuck, sweetheart. I'm taking you to the doctor. No arguments. Come on."

Taking my hand firmly, he pulled me to his side and led me into a nearby cab. I leaned on him for support, much too weak to argue, and Braydon silently held me as the cab sped away for the hospital.

20

After a battery of questions and tests from the doctor and nurses, Braydon and I waited in the cold, sterile hospital room still no closer to an answer. They wheeled a machine into the space and dimmed the lights to perform an internal ultrasound to see what was going on inside my stomach. The technician probed me with a little wand and stared intently at the image on the screen.

Our relationship changed in an instant with three little words.

"Congratulations. You're pregnant."

The floor of my stomach dropped away. I wanted to pull the bitchy ultrasound tech by her ponytail and demand someone else repeat the scan. Someone who could make sense of this alternate universe I must have entered. Braydon wasn't even my boyfriend. He'd never be okay with a baby. Then why was he looking at the screen like it was the most beautiful thing he'd ever seen?

"Can you do that again? That heartbeat thingy?" he asked. He laced his fingers between mine and squeezed.

The ultrasound tech used the uncomfortable wand once again. The little black-and-white blob on the screen danced.

"We made that, kitten. You and me," he whispered, his voice full of awe.

She adjusted a knob on the machine and the thumpity-thump sound kicked up again, insistent and sure. There was no doubting there was a baby in there. Either that or a horse was galloping in the next room. "Based on your last menstrual cycle and the measurements I've taken, you're seven weeks and four days along. Congratulations again." She removed the wand and handed me a box of tissues. "Go ahead and get cleaned up, and I'll print some of the pictures for you to take home."

Once she left the room, my head fell back to the table; I closed my eyes and tried to focus on what I knew I needed to do. I took a deep breath and began. "Braydon, I know you're probably scared—I am too. But it'll be okay. I don't expect anything from you. I have a good job, health insurance, I can support us." Me and my baby. How I could feel protective over something I'd known about for three minutes, I had no idea. "And there's day care, and my mom lives nearby in New Jersey. I'll make it work." I had to.

His silence dragged on and I finally forced my eyes open and looked at him.

His brows drew together. "No."

No? I was not giving up my baby no matter what he said.

That was out of the question. I'd do fine raising my baby alone, thank you very much. I could already see us—I'd be the cool mom in Central Park with skinny jeans and a chic diaper bag and the world's most adorable baby on my hip. My mood lifted at the thought.

"This is my baby—our baby—and I will take care of all three of us. I'm not going anywhere. No fucking way." He pressed a hand over my stomach as if to shield the baby from his curse. "Earmuffs, buddy." With his hand still resting over my belly, he continued, "My sperm is fucking amazing." His proud smile confused me. He was happy about this pregnancy?

Braydon helped me off the table and I redressed, then we sat in the chairs and waited for the doctor to return with the photos. I was still too much in shock to do anything more than sit there quietly. But Braydon couldn't seem to stop touching me, lightly rubbing my knee, holding my hand, or touching my belly. My mind flashed to our unexpected romp in Los Angeles. We'd been too caught up in the moment to use a condom.

"Move in with me," he said suddenly.

Wow. I laughed.

"What's funny?"

"I've only been to your apartment once—and now I'm being invited to move in?"

"Yes." He turned to fully face me, gazing deeply into my eyes. "I was too cautious, scared to jump in with you like I really wanted. I could tell you weren't the type I could have a casual fling with and not fall for. That fucked up all my plans."

He covered my belly with his hands once again, cringing at his curse word. "But I was being a coward. Love is messy, it's scary and overwhelming at times, but it's everything. What my parents had, I know my dad wouldn't have traded for the world, despite how it all ended. And I'm sick of denying how I feel about you."

After a soft knock, the door opened and the doctor entered. I was thankful I didn't have to respond to Bray just yet. I had no clue what to say. He was being totally irrational. The doctor sat across from us and handed me the printed black-and-white photos of my little kidney bean, and then began to cover all the prenatal dos and don'ts and what to expect during the next eight months. Basically all of life's pleasures were being stripped away from me—coffee, alcohol, soft cheeses—but exercise was still encouraged. *Ugh.* God was definitely a man.

Braydon hung on the doctor's every word and occasionally interjected with questions of his own. I felt numb and sat there bouncing my knee in silent anxiousness while I stared down at the photos in my shaking hands. While the doctor spoke, Braydon's offer hung heavily on my mind. Could we really do this? Go from a faux-couple to moving in together and raising a baby? Something told me if anyone could do this and do it with humor and ease, it'd be us. We just worked. And it seemed he was finally seeing that.

We were quiet as we left the doctor's office. The first stop was the drugstore, where we picked up gingerroot for my nausea and a bottle of prenatal vitamins, along with a tub of rocky road ice cream, which I was suddenly craving. Badly. It took every bit of willpower I had not to peel the lid off the carton on the cab ride to Braydon's and dig in with my bare fingers.

Though I hadn't agreed to anything else, I did agree to a sleepover at his place.

"You sure you don't need anything? I can lend you something to sleep in, a toothbrush, whatever you want."

"Thank you, that'll be perfect."

He smiled at me, flashing that dimpled grin and those gorgeous blue eyes and I felt calmed, like maybe everything really would be okay somehow. "So . . . dinner, yes? What are you in the mood for?" he asked.

I held up my carton of ice cream. "I'm good."

He chuckled. "Got it." Returning a moment later from the kitchen with two spoons, we settled in the living room with the tub of ice cream between us.

I almost made him suffer by refusing to share, but then decided he'd been too sweet today. I couldn't say no to him.

Over spoonfuls of ice cream, Braydon brought up the topic of me moving in again. "I know there's not a ton of extra space here, but the baby would sleep in our room for the first few months anyhow, right?"

I let him talk, nodding occasionally, but not coming right out and agreeing to anything. This was a huge step for him. He should at least sleep on it at the very least, make sure it was what he really wanted.

"Why are you being so quiet?" he finally asked.

I shrugged. "It's just a lot of change, Bray. I don't expect you to rearrange your whole life just because I got knocked up."

He released a heavy sigh and took my hands. "I need to say some things."

I nodded, meeting his eyes. I would listen to anything he had to say. Maybe he was finally coming to his senses about how much work raising a baby would be.

"It was never just sex between us, we both know that. I looked forward to seeing you, bringing you dinner, listening to stories about your day. The truth is, I'm miserable when you're not with me. You're the one I want to see every day and I can't sleep at night until you've texted me that you're in bed. I know I sound like a pussy right now, but I don't care. I've been trying to figure out a way to tell you all this for a while now, but I was worried about your reaction. I didn't want you thinking I just wanted to start having sex again. And I do, believe me, but I want all of you. No more holding back." He brought a warm palm to my cheek and stroked my bottom lip with his thumb. "God, Ellie, I'm fucking crazy about you. Your smart mouth, your intelligence, beauty . . . the way you fuck. I think I fell a little bit in love that first night with you. Which was why I fought so hard to enforce the parameters of our arrangement."

I chewed on my lip. I wanted to believe him, but I was terrified his declaration had more to do with the baby than with me. "Just because I'm pregnant doesn't mean we have to . . ."

"Stop. You think I'm just realizing this? Bringing you to

my apartment, knocking down all my walls—it was stupid—
I should have just told you, but bringing you here was my way
of showing you I wanted more with you. I just didn't want to
push you for more when I'd already pushed you away so many
times."

He sat back against the sofa, breaking our connection
and looking serious. "And I won't push you now, either. If
you want me—all of me—you have me. If you just want to be
friends, you can have that too, as long as you know I'm going
to be as involved in this baby's life as I can possibly be. And
it would be a lot easier if you moved in with me. The three of
us could be together like a real family, travel to photo shoots
together even."

I stayed silent, tears building in my eyes. It was everything
I ever wanted. I was still scared to be a mom, but excited too.
"What do you think they'd say if we brought a baby on set?"

"They'd freak at how gorgeous our kid is, obviously."

"I'm sorry, this is just a lot to process." I pressed my fingers to my temples, abandoning my spoon in the tub of melt-
ing ice cream.

He nodded. "I know. You don't have to make any decisions right now. Let's go get ready for bed. It's been a big day."

That was the understatement of the year. My day had
begun with meeting Braydon to see if we were going to rekin-
dle our friendship, then I'd helped him and Katrina put their
pasts behind them, and then came the biggest bombshell of
all—finding out I didn't have the flu after all, and instead was

expecting a baby. But the biggest news of all was that Braydon wanted more with me—much more. Asking me to move in was a total shock.

As we got ready for bed, me dressing in an oversized T-shirt of Bray's, I crawled in between his sheets. I was experiencing his soft linen sheets for the first time. It felt new and completely comfortable at the same time. Like I was meant to be here. Despite my fears that he was only being so open with me because I was pregnant, I found myself thankful that he'd invited me into his space before we knew I was expecting. It made his feelings and his declaration earlier tonight more real. It wasn't just because of the baby. It was because he'd finally realized that he and I were great together. At least I hoped so. I curled into the fluffy pillow and felt Bray crawl in beside me. His arms snaked around my middle and pulled me to him until my back was nested in against his chest. I smiled into the darkness.

"How are you feeling?" he whispered against my hair.

"Better," I whispered back. "How are you feeling?"

"Happy." He kissed the tender spot behind my ear and I felt his smile against my skin. "Goodnight, kitten."

"Night, Bray."

I drifted off to sleep, overwhelmed by all the changes of the day but feeling like with Braydon by my side, all was right.

21

As the months passed by, I became more and more excited about moving in with Braydon. We lived too far apart and since we wanted to be together every day, the distance became more and more of an annoyance. It was time. And there was no denying my place was a bit of a dump anyhow. He wouldn't let me carry a single box, even though I was still active and working out regularly.

I remained upstairs in his apartment, intercepting each box and suitcase he delivered and began the process of melding my life with his. My dresser, which sat across from his, was filled with socks, underwear, and maternity clothes; the space in his closet that he'd cleared held my work clothes; and the bathroom . . . well there was no denying that my toiletries, makeup, and hair items completely overtook his bathroom. Braydon didn't seem to mind at all. He moved his shaving cream and deodorant onto the windowsill and let me have my way with his bathroom cabinets.

He even made room on his living room shelf for all my favorite books—including the ones with buff shirtless guys on them. Now that was love.

"Last box, babe." Braydon hoisted the cardboard box over his head as he crossed the threshold and toed the door closed behind him. After depositing the box labeled "Kitchen Stuff" on the counter, he joined me on the couch.

As it so often did these days, Braydon's hand came to a rest on my belly. "Still no kicking?"

I shook my head. "I'm not quite four months yet, so the doctor said that's normal." I knew Braydon was excited to feel the baby move, but I'd read that typically happened between four and five months. "Soon enough." I patted his hand. I was still nervous about the whole giving-birth thing, but I'd come to accept my new outlook on life. I was even excited to see Braydon as a dad. Since the day we met for coffee, and found out I was pregnant, he'd been there for me every step of the way. He'd been my rock, attended every doctor's appointment, stocked up his apartment with prenatal vitamins, stuffed animals, and baby-proofing materials even though I told him we had a while before we needed those.

"You know what today is, right?" Braydon smiled like he knew a secret I didn't.

"Um, no. What?"

"For starters, it's the six-month anniversary of Emmy and Ben's wedding."

"Oh. That's cool."

"Which means it's our six-month anniversary, too."

I chuckled. "Maybe the anniversary of you going down on me."

"Exactly, and from that very first taste you were mine." I couldn't deny what he said wasn't true. I was his, right from the very beginning. He lifted me from the couch and set me on his lap. "I'm so glad you said yes and that you're here, kitten."

I laid my head on his shoulder and inhaled the unique scent that was just Bray. "Me too." I shifted so I could meet his eyes. "You know . . . the nickname kitten is awfully close to Kat—your ex's name." I frowned.

His eyebrows shot up. "I never realized, but you're right. So no more kitten, then?"

I shook my head. "Nope."

"Hmm." He touched his forehead to mine. "How about Mrs. Kincaid then? Would that suit you?"

I blinked at him, utterly speechless.

Epilogue
Braydon

I loved watching Ellie like this. Her cheeks were rosy and pink from the cold and her fingers were stretched out, reaching for our daughter. "Come on, you can do it," she encouraged. Brayleigh let go of her grasp around my index finger and let out a little squeal as she toddled toward her pretty momma. She was just starting to take her first shaky steps when she had assistance or something to hold on to. It was amazing to see.

"What a big girl," Emmy commented, bouncing their baby boy, Mace, on her hip. He was so bundled up he looked like the Michelin Man. But I wouldn't make the mistake of telling Emmy that again. Seriously, though, what were they feeding that kid, bacon? He quietly sucked on a pacifier and watched Brayleigh with wide eyes.

The last couple of years of my life were anything but expected. I met Ellie and was immediately attracted to her sassy attitude and quick wit. Not to mention her beauty. Her dark hair was currently pinned up and loose strands were rustling around her face in the breeze. It was early spring, and while there was still a pile of snow blanketing the city, the sun was shining brightly overhead and we were enjoying some much overdue outdoor time at the park.

"Are you guys ready to get some breakfast?" Emmy asked.

"Let's do it." I lifted Brayleigh into my arms and her surprised little giggle melted my heart.

Ben took Mace from Emmy and placed him in his luxury stroller. Seriously, that thing was nicer than my first car.

Breakfast out together had become a Sunday morning tradition for us over the past year. When Emmy had gotten pregnant a few months after Ellie, Ben and I had been at the mercy of their cravings, and this diner we'd stumbled across had quite the eclectic menu. They could order anything from blueberry pancakes to tuna salad to beef stroganoff no matter the time of day. And it was kid friendly, which meant even after the babies were born, we'd continued our tradition.

As we set off down the sidewalk, I tucked Ellie's hand inside the warmth of my jacket and pressed a kiss to her lips. "You cold?"

"Not too bad." She wedged herself closer, opening my jacket to nestle in against my side. Her hand drifted lower down my abs.

"No copping a feel in public, Mrs. Kincaid," I warned.

"I'm glad to see having a baby hasn't changed you two." Emmy rolled her eyes as she pushed Mace alongside us.

Not a thing had cooled between me and Ellie. If anything, watching her with our daughter only made me love her more. She was so loving, so patient, so sweet with Brayleigh that it stole my breath. Though she sometimes complained that she rarely had time to get ready, put on makeup, and get dressed in something that wasn't covered in baby drool, she'd never looked more beautiful to me. I loved watching her sit and feed the baby, cooing sweet little nonsense words as she gazed down into our daughter's inquisitive blue eyes.

We entered the diner and made our way toward our usual booth as Ben grabbed two highchairs from the front, carrying one in each arm back to our spot. We had dining out with two small infants down to a science.

I slid Brayleigh into a highchair and her chubby little hands immediately began slapping down against the tray. Mace watched her, flashing a silly toothless grin, and began imitating her, slapping his own tray. Ellie pulled a plastic container of cereal from her purse and dumped some onto each tray.

Since we no longer needed to consult the menus here, we sat watching the babies babble and play. Brayleigh picked up a Cheerio and held it out to Mace's open mouth.

"Look at that, she's feeding him." Ellie smiled proudly.

"Our little girl is obviously going to be awesome—I mean, look at her. She'll be top of her class, an academic all-star, a cellist . . . no a pianist," I said.

Emmy giggled. "Passionate about penis just like her mom."

"I hate to break it to you, but in eighteen years, my son is gonna be balls deep in your daughter," Ben said, looking me squarely in the eye.

"No, dude. My daughter's not dating until she's forty." Fuck that.

Ben laughed. "I didn't say anything about dating."

"No way, she's not going out with guys like us."

"What? We turned out all right. We wised up and got the girls in the end, didn't we?"

Emmy and Ellie were watching our exchange, shaking their heads. I laced Ellie's fingers in between mine. She was still getting used to the big rock I'd put on her finger. She twisted it around constantly fidgeting with it. I had gotten my act together just in time. Looking back, I was surprised she'd given me so many second chances. I guess she'd known all along how good things could be between us. She might have thought I was rushing things—moving her into my apartment, proposing, and then marrying her last spring when she was pregnant, but when you know, you know. It was advice my dad had given me, and he'd been spot on. I'd never been more certain about anything than having this amazing girl in my life. Thank God I'd come to my senses. I couldn't imagine missing out on all this.

Brayleigh might have come as a surprise, but she'd enriched our lives in ways we never could have imagined. Caring for a tiny, helpless person brought a deeper meaning, a sense of purpose, to my life that wasn't there before.

Ben met my eyes and I knew he was thinking the same

thing. Our lives had changed drastically. Instead of dining in five-star restaurants and discussing the wine list, we were at a tiny diner with Formica floors where our kids' spilled food could easily be swept up.

As I watched Ellie cut a waffle and sausage link into tiny bits, I couldn't help lifting her mouth to mine. "I love you," I whispered against her lips. I didn't know if it was because I'd waited so long to tell her, or maybe because we had a child together, but either way, I felt emotions more intensely now, and I didn't keep things to myself.

Her eyes flashed quizzically on mine. "I love you, too."

Ben chuckled. "All right you two. Cool it. Seriously, there's no way your daughter's waiting until she's forty to date. She's got your genes. She'll be a horn dog. It runs in the family."

"Excuse me," Ellie injected, turning to fully face Ben. "You're one to talk. You two . . ." She raised her eyebrows, waggling a finger between Ben and Emmy. "You two are worse. You joined the mile-high club during our Christmas flight to Aspen while we babysat your son."

Emmy's cheeks went pink. Seriously? She had to realize that everyone on that plane knew what was happening in the first-class lavatory. They were loud as hell. I laughed out loud and Brayleigh mimicked me, giggling along.

"Is that funny, Brayleigh Mae?" Ellie asked, kissing our daughter's chubby outstretched fingers.

God, I loved my wife. I loved how she could put someone in their place, how she lived life to the fullest without holding back, and how she loved with her whole heart. I was a lucky man.

"Yes, and how did you guys get together?" Emmy challenged, tapping her fingers against her chin. "Oh yeah, that's right. You went down on my maid of honor in a bathroom stall at my wedding. That's superclassy. So much better than doing it on a plane."

I shrugged. "Hey, she's fucking delicious. I can't be held responsible for that. Next time don't have such a tasty maid of honor."

"Bray!" Ellie swatted my shoulder and shot me a glare before sliding the chopped-up waffles and sausage onto Brayleigh's tray.

"Cheers to delicious wives." Ben raised his coffee mug to mine.

"I'll drink to that." Brayleigh hoisted her sippy cup in the air, wanting me to clink hers next. "Yeah, mommy's delicious, huh?"

"Heaven help me," Ellie muttered, watching us.

However our relationship had started, I knew we were meant to last and it filled me with a deeper sense of happiness than I'd ever known.

Acknowledgments

To the readers who have followed this series, which began with Ben and Emmy, I want to thank you for your support. And to the new readers, thank you for taking a chance on Bray and Ellie!

Thank you to my lovely editor, Jhanteigh, at Atria Books for your wisdom and guidance regarding this series. It was lovely working with you!

I would like to thank my early readers for your feedback and enthusiasm. To Heather, Sali, Christine, and most notably Ellie. Thank you for letting me borrow your name.

To John. You're my everything. Xo.